CRUX

DRAGON BRIDES

KATE RUDOLPH

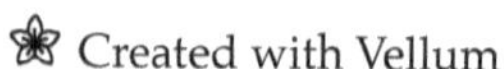 Created with Vellum

ABOUT CRUX

Prince Crux is in a bind.

When the Dragon King commands Crux find a mate, his days of carefree bachelorhood are over. One trip to a psychic matchmaker and he's on the path to his destiny. But it all comes screeching to a halt when he meets a human woman who lights his inner fire and makes him yearn.

She's got a pair of roller skates and an attitude.

Courtney is supposed to be putting the shambles of her life back together. Getting abducted by aliens isn't part of the plan. Neither is getting rescued by a scorchingly hot dragon that makes her think of an impossible future. But they have no chance together if they can't first escape a planet full of monsters intent on their destruction.

Fated mates, fierce women, and dragon princes are ready to find their mates in the new Dragon Brides series from Kate Rudolph.

Courtney Lamb's feet were heavy, and she had the headache to end all headaches. She curled into herself on one side, trying to scrunch up into a ball, but her feet dragged along the floor and noise echoed off the metal walls around her.

She was still wearing her roller skates.

How? She always took them off before leaving work. She couldn't exactly drive with wheels on her feet. And yet, as she turned over and pulled her legs in, they slipped on the cold metal floor.

Where was she? This wasn't the root beer stand she worked at, nor was it the creepy, decrepit steel barn that sat on the very edge of the restaurant property. She looked around, squinting in the dim light and trying to get her bearings.

It was industrial, but the room was small. Steel

walls. No windows. And a weird echo-y noise in the distance that might have been an air conditioner.

She didn't see a door.

Courtney scrambled to her knees before realizing she wasn't going to get far with roller skates on her feet. She shucked the skates off and wiggled her toes in her sweaty socks before tying the laces together. No matter what was going on, she didn't want to lose her skates.

They were expensive. And one of the few nice things she had left.

There was a shriek down the hall, or at least, Courtney assumed there was a hall, and she flinched.

What the hell was going on?

Had she been kidnapped? Was she being trafficked? She'd seen plenty of Facebook posts talking about the perils of being a woman in America, but most of it seemed like a bunch of bullshit. People didn't *actually* hide under cars to slit the Achilles tendons of the unsuspecting.

Right?

She ran a hand down the back of her leg, as if to assure herself that she was intact. Obviously she was. Other than the headache, she wasn't hurt.

She was just confused.

And in trouble.

She wanted to call for help, but a second scream from somewhere in the building made her throat freeze up. No, she didn't want to call attention to herself.

With her skate laces tied together, she was able to sling her skates over her shoulder and get to her feet. The room seemed even tinier when she was standing up. Was she a prisoner? Why?

Her mom was going to kill her when she found out.

Of course, Courtney hadn't spoken to her mother in months, and now was not the time to think about how this would impact her mother's career. She was in the middle of an abduction, she had to care about herself.

She stroked the top of her skate, half for comfort, half to remind herself that it was sturdy and could probably be used as some kind of weapon.

She was wearing the thick leggings and short sleeve red tunic that made up her work uniform, though her name badge must have fallen off somewhere. That furthered Courtney's theory that she'd been taken from work.

She couldn't remember clocking out. She wracked her brain, but the last thing she remembered was telling her co-worker, Sarah, that she didn't have any plans for the weekend. The same as every weekend these days.

That wasn't what she should be feeling bad about at the moment.

Was Sarah a trafficker? Had she waited to strike until Courtney was at her most vulnerable?

No. That was ridiculous. Sarah was a college student trying to make ends meet. She wasn't sinister.

Where was the freaking door?

Courtney whirled around, but she still didn't see anything that looked like it would let her out of the room. She was in a metal tomb and she couldn't escape.

Her breaths came faster and faster, and black spots danced in front of her eyes.

No. No. Now was not the time for a panic attack.

She hadn't had one in months, and she didn't want them to restart. They sucked.

And so did her whole situation.

"Think of the good things," she commanded herself. There weren't many. But she had to number them off. "I'm in my regular clothes. My skates are fine. I'm not hurt." She ran out of optimism after that. Any other "good" news sounded like asking for trouble, and Courtney wasn't interested in that.

She ran her hands over the metal walls, looking for a seam that might reveal a hidden door. There had to be something. She had been put in the room, so there had to be a way to get her out of it. She looked up, wondering if she'd somehow been lowered in, but the ceiling was too high to make out any fine detail in the dim light.

Where was the light even coming from?

There wasn't a ceiling light. She didn't see lights in the floor. There was just a faint, pale blue glow all around her that allowed her to see.

It was another good thing, and Courtney decided not to question it.

She had her skates, but she wished she had a skate tool. That fancy little wrench might have helped her pry an invisible door open. But her skate tool and spare wheels were in her bag at work. Along with her cell phone, a bit of cash, and her car keys. She had no way to contact anyone for help.

And *there* was the hyperventilation.

She tried to control her breathing, but the walls felt like they were closing in. She heard footsteps coming her way and shrank back as far away from the sound as she could. The room was maybe six feet wide. She couldn't shrink back much.

A brave woman would have done something. Courtney *wished* she was brave. But she couldn't think and she wanted to live. She was pretty sure brave people died quicker than cowards.

The wall opposite her glowed a faint yellow, and a rectangle formed before sliding to one side, the invisible door revealing itself. A brave woman would have charged.

Instead, Courtney watched a monster step inside.

It—and it was clearly an *it*, not a person—was some kind of *creature*. Over eight feet tall, antennae coming out of its head, and sinister purple skin that was covered in a faint slime. It wore clothes over most of its body, but its arms were exposed, and scars or tattoos or something covered it.

One of its hands wasn't a hand at all. Instead, it came to a fine point and had an edge that made it look like a sword.

It looked like something out of *Star Trek*.

And she was wearing a red shirt.

Shit.

It wore pants, but judging by the giant bulge right where his dick should be, he didn't plan on wearing them for long. And she didn't want to find out if his dick was a knife too.

Working by instinct, not pausing to think, Courtney grabbed onto one of her skates and swung, sending the other one flying at the monster's head. He didn't expect it, and the wheels, metal plate, and carbon fiber boot were enough to send him slumping to the ground.

Oh god, was he dead? Had she broken her skate?

Courtney flailed for a moment and cut off the horrible noise that tried to escape her throat. She checked her skate first. Except for a bit of slime and something that might have been monster blood, it seemed fine.

Good.

She didn't know how to check for a pulse on a monster. She didn't know if she wanted him to be dead or alive.

Oh god. What was she going to do?

She had to run.

She stepped around the monster and dove through the door, just in case it tried to close. The hallway was narrow and lit up by the same ambient blue light as her cell. She chose a direction and ran, unsure if it was correct but refusing to hesitate.

She stumbled when she passed a window.

Courtney came to a halt and looked outside.

She expected a city. Maybe some trees. *Something.*

Instead, she saw the black of space.

Outer space.

She wasn't in a warehouse. She was on a space ship, and they were hovering above some planet that didn't look like Earth.

How was she going to get home?

She was trying to think, then something impacted the ship, and Courtney stumbled as the lights went out and all of her senses went haywire.

2

Prince Crux grinned at his brothers, Saber and Ranger, and beckoned them forward with the claws on his hand. His armor was up and fire raged inside of him, ready to burst free.

He wouldn't use it, of course. Calling on fire during a sparring match was bad form and he'd never hear the end of it.

No, he was going to beat his brothers fair and square.

Saber and Ranger were equally distant from him, and both were breathing hard. The fight had been going on for nearly half an hour, and they all knew Crux was winning. He always did.

And his brothers weren't about to change that.

He tipped his head back and laughed with the joy

of the fight. Battle called to him, and he wanted to charge.

If he was in his other form, he would bat his wings and soar, raining fire down on his enemies and clashing in the sky with whoever opposed him.

But Saber and Ranger weren't defeated yet. Crux was too busy laughing to see his brothers exchange a look or read the plan that formed silently between them. The two of them charged, and Crux had to dart away to avoid being taken down to the dirt.

It was on.

And now he felt the challenge.

Working together, Saber and Ranger were an actual threat, and as the minutes ticked by, Crux began to worry his winning streak might be coming to an end. His face was smudged with dirt from a lucky hit, and his muscles were starting to cry out from heavy use.

He wanted more.

But before he could make a counter move and show his brothers exactly where they stood, a gong sounded, calling the sparring session to an end. Ranger skidded, colliding into Crux, and they both tumbled to the ground.

Saber punched a hand in the air. "I'm victorious. Last dragon standing."

"The stars deceive you, brother." Crux and Ranger got to their feet, and judging by the look Ranger was shooting him, the two of them were ready to team up against Saber.

Last dragon standing. Ha!

A servant stood beside the gong, holding onto the mallet, a worried look on his face, as if he wasn't sure he should strike it again.

Crux checked the time. "Our session is not scheduled to end for another turn of the dial, Yotar. What is it?" He wanted to fight more, but Yotar wouldn't stop them for something trivial.

"The king has requested your presence, my prince," Yotar said with a slight bow. "He instructs me to inform you that the younger princes are welcome to continue to train."

Crux didn't like the sound of that, and his first instinct was to let Yotar know it. But Yotar was a servant and merely the messenger. Crux leashed his anger and let his form bleed away so that he was fully a man. In peace time, it could be seen as an act of aggression to approach the king in warrior form. And he didn't want his father to think that he was scheming to take the throne early.

No. Crux was more than happy to leave his father to rule while he lived his own happy life.

"I shall attend him once I've showered off this muck," he said, gesturing to his face.

Yotar's lips flattened into a thin line of

disapproval. No doubt the king wanted to see Crux immediately.

There was no winning. If Crux didn't wash, his father would censure him for being dirty. If he did, he'd be censured for making the king wait. So rather than take a relaxing dip in the royal baths, Crux wiped himself off quickly and splashed scented water on his hair to cover most of the scent of sweat.

It would have to do.

Not ten minutes later, he was presenting himself in the throne room and its empty throne. Still, Crux bowed. Who knew if his father was watching?

A side door opened, and his father stepped out as Crux stood. He beckoned Crux over to his private office, and once Crux was inside, closed the door behind him.

So it was to be a private upbraiding. Crux tried to think of what he'd done wrong recently, but nothing came to mind. Well, there had been the prank with the water bucket over Saber's door, but that was nothing.

"Sit," commanded King Venin as he took a seat behind his giant desk. This was where most of his work actually happened. Here and at the desks of the countless clerks and advisors who made the kingdom function.

Crux sat. He kept quiet, waiting for his father to name his grievance.

He didn't. "You were sparring with your brothers."

"Training comes along well," Crux confirmed. "They will honor the army one day as true dragon warriors."

King Venin nodded in agreement. "That is not why I wanted to speak with you."

Of course not. But Crux wasn't stupid enough to say that out loud. "Is that so?"

The king steepled his fingers in front of him while resting his elbows on the desk. "You've stalled for long enough. It's time you took a mate. I'm sick of having two sons who refuse to do their duty. At least your youngest brother has taken my advice on the matter."

Crux had known this was coming. His thirtieth birthday had just passed. His father had sired all three of his sons by the time he was Crux's age. It didn't make Crux any more eager to find a mate for himself. "Have you chosen a woman for me?" It had always been a possibility. Crux was the crown prince and his father's heir. Choosing his own mate was not necessarily his right.

Surprisingly, his father shook his head. "This is your final chance. You have until the next full moon to present your desired mate to me for my approval." He stared at Crux for a moment, daring him to make a challenge.

His father no doubt wanted the challenge. If Crux complained, his father would rip the condition away and present Crux with someone who would make the aristocracy happy.

Someone Crux couldn't stand.

It wasn't that there was anything *wrong* with the ladies of the kingdom. It was that Crux was a warrior and had nothing in common with them. And the ladies who fought in the army were not the kind of ladies his father would approve of.

Crux didn't argue. He could feel his choices beginning to slip through his fingers, but he refused to ruin his chance so early. There had to be at least *one* lady out there who he could stand to mate with.

Perhaps his fated mate.

He couldn't let the hope show on his face. It was the kind of fancy his father would scoff at.

"Be gone," his father finally said. "I am busy."

Crux left. He headed back towards the training grounds, and his brothers attempted to summon him back for another match. Crux considered it for a moment before turning abruptly and heading out of the palace and down into Dragon City.

He thought of every lady he knew, and he knew many, but none of them had managed to spark his interest. They all knew he was a prince and what mating with him would mean. He'd never felt like so much meat as when he attended parties with scheming ladies intent on the Dragon Crown.

That was the problem of his position. No one wanted him for *him*. They wanted his rank or his coin or his favor.

But there had to be someone.

The streets weren't too crowded as he walked. Dragon City was not the largest settlement in the kingdom, despite the castle. Or perhaps because of it. The king's guard liked to make sure the city was safe for the royals who lived there and could make things… uncomfortable at times for the residents of the city. But it was why Crux was safe enough walking alone and no one gave him a second look.

He didn't know what made him stop. He was on a market street full of shops. Some sold weapons. Others entertainment devices. And if his nose did not deceive him, he was near food stalls of some kind.

But that wasn't what caught his attention.

He read the sign on the window: Royal Matchmaker.

He could question the validity of the claim. As far as he knew, his father and brothers had never approached a matchmaker in their lives. There were other ways to find mates.

But Crux had heard of this matchmaker. It was said she wasn't just good, she was unnaturally good. A psychic.

If he had a fated mate out there, perhaps she could point him towards her.

It was crazy. Crux was a prince, he didn't need a matchmaker.

But he only had until the next full moon to make the choice on his own. And a true leader knew when it was time to ask for help.

He looked at the door for several long seconds and almost continued down the street. It was madness to even consider it.

But his father had driven him to madness, and he was running out of choices.

Crux reached for the door, ready to greet his fate.

3

IF COURTNEY NEEDED any more proof that she was in space, it came when she started floating. Whatever was keeping gravity going failed, and she found herself plastered to the ceiling and reaching for the wall, trying to orient herself.

She saw streaks of yellow outside the nearest window, and sweat coated her arms. It was getting hot and they were crashing.

Gravity came back with a jolt, and Courtney knew she didn't have much time. She needed to brace herself before they made impact.

Not that it would matter.

She was going to die.

But she couldn't give up hope. She scrambled down the hall and let out a cry of relief when she found a fold down chair with easy-to-use restraints.

She climbed into it and secured herself with shaking hands.

Then everything was shaking.

Then there was a crash.

And then it was scarily silent.

Courtney didn't hear anyone screaming this time. She didn't know how *she* was alive. Maybe she wasn't. Maybe she'd been dead the entire time and this was hell.

Except it didn't really feel like hell, not what she'd imagined anyway.

She thought her roller skates had managed to wrap around her neck and reached up to adjust them. But the skates were hanging on her shoulder.

There was a giant metal collar around her neck.

Courtney couldn't stop the panicked sound that escaped her throat.

Somehow that made this whole thing all the more real. She was on some kind of space ship and the scary aliens had put a collar on her and she was so far from home she had no hope of ever getting back.

She didn't have time to be amazed at finding out aliens were real.

And she couldn't stick around for more of them to find her.

Courtney undid her harness and reached up again at the collar, trying to pry it off. It didn't budge.

Frustrated tears pricked at her eyes, and hyperventilation threatened again.

She made herself take a deep breath. Then another. She didn't know what the collar did, but clearly it didn't control her. She'd been able to walk out of her cell without anyone stopping her, *and* she'd bashed that alien's head in.

Did that count as murder?

Not thinking about it.

She'd worry about getting the collar off once she was off the ship. If the aliens couldn't see her, they couldn't control her collar. She hoped.

Walking around now was riskier than it had been before, and she was super conscious of her sock clad feet. Pieces of metal and other debris had become dislodged in the crash, and Courtney had to step carefully to make sure she didn't hurt herself.

She heard a woman screaming as she passed down the hall and couldn't keep walking. She had to try to help.

She looked for a panel or something on the wall that would make the door appear, but she didn't recognize anything. There was weird alien writing, but she couldn't read it. And for all she knew, it wasn't writing at all, but a strange decoration.

She banged one of her skates against the wall, hoping force would do the trick. It didn't, and the woman behind the door only screamed harder.

Courtney didn't say anything. She didn't know if the woman could hear her and she was afraid to make too much noise.

And then she heard trampling footsteps coming her way fast.

Courtney looked at the wall and winced. "I'm sorry," she whispered to the woman behind the door. Then she ran. She wasn't letting the aliens catch her again.

Running in bare feet on a space ship that was falling apart was a terrible idea. Worse than walking on Legos, and she was sure her feet were bleeding and her socks torn to shreds. She tried to push the pain out of her mind, but Courtney had never been good at that.

It had one benefit. She was so focused on the pain in her feet that she couldn't worry about the aliens behind her.

She gasped for breath as she ran, and then something occurred to her. Could she even breathe the air outside? She was on some foreign planet millions—maybe billions—of miles from home. Why would the air be breathable?

But she could already see cracks in the hull of the ship. It definitely wasn't airtight anymore. So she had to hope she was lucky. Anyway, it would probably be better to suffocate than to suffer whatever the aliens wanted to do to her.

The hallway seemed to go on forever. Courtney kept moving, but she wasn't getting anywhere, until, suddenly, she did. It wasn't a door. These aliens didn't seem to like doors, but the wall had torn away to reveal barren wood that might have once been a tree and dark dirt.

The sky in the distance was bright and blue, with the slightest green tinge, but it almost looked like Earth.

How was she going to get back to Earth?

Courtney carefully stepped out of the ship and onto the soft ground, her feet practically weeping with thanks. The ground was a little damp, and that would be an issue later.

If there was a later.

But Courtney needed a plan. The aliens were bound to exit the ship eventually, and if they found her, she was a goner. What were the chances that there was a civilization of not-evil aliens on this planet?

Well, there was a tree, and dirt, and water. Those were things that life needed, if she remembered anything from high school biology correctly. There was life of some kind on this planet. Now she had to figure out if it was the kind that had figured out space travel.

She really hoped that if there were other aliens here, they were nice.

Courtney moved carefully, both because there was plenty of ship debris on the ground and because she was sure one of the evil aliens was going to burst out of the ship at any minute. She considered picking up a bit of debris to use as a knife, but figured her skates were the better option. They'd already taken out one alien, so she hoped they could handle more.

If it came to that.

This whole thing had to be a nightmare. The kind of bad dream that made it so she couldn't sleep for a week. As Courtney took gasping breaths of the planet's air, she tried to force herself to wake up. This wasn't possible. Aliens didn't exist. Space travel didn't exist.

This wasn't real.

She squeezed her eyes shut, determined to prove it was all fake.

But her socks were getting wet from the damp dirt, and she could hear the ship creaking and falling apart next to her. The place smelled like the green of fresh air after a rainstorm mixed with the spilled gas scent of a gas station. Not exactly pleasant, but somehow familiar.

There was nothing else familiar about this.

"Move," she commanded herself. "Do it." She couldn't sit around and cry. Even if this was just a dream and her alarm rescued her at any moment, she couldn't let herself surrender to despair. "They can't have me."

She moved, but slowly. She took two quick steps and nearly impaled herself on a nasty spike of debris. After that, Courtney's pace slowed to a crawl. She made it around the corner of the ship and saw dense foliage and a mountain range further beyond it. She could hide in the forest, she hoped. And maybe find water or food.

Her stomach grumbled at the thought. Food hadn't been on her mind at all when she woke up, but she wasn't sure the last time she'd eaten, and her body was starting to protest.

Well, her body was going to have to deal with it.

Courtney crept along, trying to get away from the ship and hoping none of the aliens saw her. She thought she'd made it until the collar around her throat started to tighten and she froze, gripping it, trying to loosen it.

She wrenched her head around and saw an alien standing in the wreckage of the ship pointing something at her. He jerked his hand towards her, but she refused to be summoned, even if she couldn't breathe.

Better to suffocate. That had been her thought before. It was a lot harder to hold onto the conviction when her airway was cut off.

She grasped onto one skate, ready to launch the

pair of them at the alien in a desperate attempt for freedom. But he was thirty feet away. There was no way she could launch the skates that far, not even if she could gasp in a full breath.

It was over.

Black spots danced in front of her eyes, and her legs went wobbly. If she tried to move, she'd fall over. Hell, she was sure she couldn't stand for much longer.

Her ears popped and a bright light flashed behind her. If she had any strength left, she would have turned around to look, but instead she saw a blast of something shoot over her shoulder and hit the alien square in the chest. He tumbled to the ground and the choking hold on her neck let go.

Courtney sucked in a breath and looked at her savior. He was haloed in bright light and looked like a human man. He held out a hand as the bright light behind him faded. "Come on. Let's get out of here."

4

THERE WAS no way Crux would find his mate on this planet, no matter what the matchmaker said. This was no place for a lady dragon. But he couldn't just step back through the portal to home and leave the human in front of him struggling with a slave collar around her neck.

He hated slavers. They were the scum of the universe. He was going to make these ones pay for wasting his time. After he rescued as many people as he could from their care.

The human prisoner had dark hair that was held back from her face and pale skin. Dark eyes with dark smudges under them, and the kind of curves that would make him think sinful thoughts if he wasn't in the middle of a mission to find his mate. She wore a long red tunic and dark leggings, and for some reason she had wheeled shoes hanging over one shoulder rather than on her feet.

Crux had never been to Earth, but he'd met a few humans. None of them wore shoes like that.

"Were there other prisoners on the ship?" he asked as he led her away from the debris and to the edge of the forest. They didn't have a lot of cover, but it was better than standing in the open. He had the feeling she couldn't make it far.

A feeling that was confirmed when she slumped down to sit on a large rock beside a short tree. She breathed deep, her hands shaking before she balled them into fists and then rested them on her legs, fingers gripping her knees hard enough to bruise. "I heard a woman screaming," she said. "I couldn't help her. I tried. But I couldn't open the door. And they were coming down the hall. What's happening? Who are they? Where am I?" She looked up at him with pleading eyes.

Crux's heart went out to her. Slavers loved to take people from planets that weren't yet sophisticated enough for interstellar travel. The panic and dismay was enough to crush most spirits. "I realize this is all hard to take in, but you're safe now." He held up his teleporter and waved the device at her. "I can send you back to my home and then once I've dealt with this issue, I'll send you back to Earth. You *are* from Earth, right?" Humans had been abducted from that planet ever since they'd evolved, and there were quite a few settlements around the galaxy full of them. But those humans normally weren't so disturbed by the thought of capture.

Her eyes got wide, and she shook her head in disbelief. "Of course I'm from Earth. Where the hell are you from? Who the hell are you?" She squeezed her legs even tighter, and Crux had the strangest urge to reach out and comfort her.

Maybe his father was right. Maybe he did need a mate. "My name is Crux. What's yours?" He spoke in his gentlest tone, the kind he'd use with a scared animal. He didn't want this woman bolting and running right back towards the slavers.

"*What* the hell are you?" she demanded.

He was pretty sure that wasn't her name. But she was scared and grasping for any control over the situation she could find. He'd dealt with scared victims before, and he would give her as much time as he could to deal. "I'm a dragon." Obviously. Hadn't she seen him shoot his fire at the slaver who'd been choking her? "What's your name?" Slavers often stripped their victims of their names, but it took a long time for names to be forgotten completely, and this woman didn't act like she'd been a slave all that long.

After all, she'd run. That was one of the first things that got beaten out of the victims.

Her breathing stuttered, and tears leaked out of her eyes. "I'm Courtney. I want to go home."

Crux's heart broke for her, just a little. "I can't send you home yet. But I can send you somewhere safe until then. Will you let me?" He didn't want to give her a choice, and he'd shove her through the portal if he had to, but it was better if the decision was hers.

She looked at him for a long moment, and he could see her stoking her inner fire. She wasn't a dragon, but she was tough. "Okay."

Thank the skies.

"This will only take a moment." He punched in the coordinates and the portal opened. "Step through. Tell whoever you meet first that Prince Crux sent you and that I'll return once I've dealt with the slave ship. Have an infirmary readied."

Courtney's eyes got wide. "Prince?"

Crux grinned. "Guilty. Now go." Under other circumstances, he might have given her a playful shove, but he doubted the human would take that well.

Courtney pushed herself to her feet and took a deep breath before stepping towards the portal. But instead of stepping through, she ran straight into it and bounced back as if it were a solid wall. That didn't stop her from trying again.

And failing again.

Crux closed the portal before she could try a third time.

"Why didn't it work?" She didn't sound angry, not exactly.

Crux was. Keeping her safe while fighting the slavers would be hard enough. But he had an idea. "Your collar. I'd wager that it prevents you from being rescued through a portal. Perhaps from getting too far from your captors. We'll need to get it off of you before I send you back."

She sank back down onto the rock and reached up to stroke the offending collar before grabbing her wheeled shoes and clutching them close to her chest. "You can't just take it off? I tried pulling it."

Crux approached slowly to take a look. He found the clasp and worked it with his fingers before shifting to his warrior form to try his claws. He shifted back when it didn't work and stepped back into Courtney's line of sight. "It looks like it requires a special tool. There should be one on the ship." He had to make a plan quickly. The slavers were bound to come this way soon. He only hoped there wasn't a tracking beacon in the collar as well. "Let's find a place to stash you, and then I'll head to the ship to find a tool. You'll be in my palace by nightfall."

That startled a laugh out of her. "Palace. Fuck. I must be hallucinating. This can't be real. How can I even understand you? Dragon? Yeah, right."

He held out a hand towards her face but didn't touch her. "May I?" He gestured towards her ear.

Courtney glared at him, but finally gave a cautious nod.

He reached behind her ear and ran his fingers over her silky skin. She shivered under his touch, and those unbidden sinful thoughts came back. Crux swiftly shoved them aside. Even if he wasn't on the lookout for his mate, this woman wouldn't be for him. She was too traumatized, too raw. She needed safety, not his lust.

Once his fingers ran over the ridges of the translator, he pulled back. "It's not uncommon for slavers to implant translators on their victims."

She reached behind her ear to feel for herself. "That sounds expensive."

"It's cruel. It gives them another excuse to beat their victims since the victims understand them perfectly well." And it was one reason that Crux would make sure no slaver walked off this planet alive. "Come on, let's find a place for you to hide."

"You're going to leave me alone?" She stepped close to him, reached out, then tore her hand back as if she couldn't stand to touch him. "That's not safe."

"It's safer than taking you back to that ship." This kind of land was bound to be full of caves and warrens, the perfect place for a human to hide for a bit.

But before they could move out, something crashed through the woods and two slavers burst through the trees. Crux dove in front of Courtney, calling up his warrior form without a thought and absorbing the blow from his blaster. The slavers weren't shooting to kill, not when they could get their merchandise back.

It was the last mistake they would make.

Crux shot a blast of fire and hit one of the slavers dead on, but the other managed to jump out of the way and closer to him and Courtney. Before Crux could change the trajectory of his flame, the second slaver got a shot off, the blast strong enough to make Crux stumble back.

The slaver was too close to Courtney for Crux to use his flame again, but he wasn't letting him take her.

Neither, it seemed, was Courtney. She grabbed onto her wheeled shoes and swung with all of her might, bashing him in the head and sending him crumpling to the ground.

Crux blasted him with fire for good measure.

Maybe this human wasn't just a victim. She had some warrior deep inside of her.

Her eyes flashed over to him, taking in his warrior form. There was an expression he couldn't quite read in her eyes. Curiosity? Lust? Whatever it was, it couldn't matter. More slavers would be coming.

Courtney slung her weapon over her shoulder and met his eyes. "I need shoes."

"Then shoes you shall have."

5

AN ALIEN DRAGON with fire powers was protecting her from evil insectoid aliens who wanted to enslave her. No matter how many times Courtney ran that thought through her mind, it didn't make any more sense.

She was pretty sure this wasn't a nightmare. Nightmares were never this vivid. Maybe she was suffering a psychotic break and was chained to a bed in a mental ward.

That wasn't a pleasant thought.

Then again, it was probably preferable to her current state.

Without much other choice, she followed after Crux as he led her back towards the ship. Why had she made a fuss about being left alone? The closer they got to the place she'd just escaped from, the crazier it sounded that she'd agreed to go back.

She stepped on a particularly pointy twig and bit back a hiss of pain. Shoes. She needed them with great urgency. Shoes and to get the stupid collar off her neck.

The ship came into view quickly, and Courtney tried to keep her breathing even. This place was going to haunt her nightmares for the rest of her life. She only hoped she had enough life left for it *to* haunt.

Crux— *Prince Crux*— held up a hand, and Courtney stopped before she ran into him. A dragon *prince*. Yeah, there was no way this was anything more than an insanely detailed hallucination. Though she hadn't realized her imagination was capable of thinking of things like this.

Between one blink and the next, he shifted from looking like a normal if insanely hot guy to a guy with weird scales on his exposed skin, claws on his hands, and a strange angularity to his features. On any other day, it would scare Courtney, but today she had run out of the ability to be shocked and could do nothing more than go with the flow.

"I don't see anyone," he said quietly and waved her forward. "We go slow. Do you have any idea how many there are?"

She stroked her fingers over her skate, half for

comfort, half to remind herself that she wasn't unarmed. "Not a clue."

That didn't surprise him, so they moved forward.

Crux seemed to know his way around the ship, and it made Courtney wonder if she'd fallen out of the hands of one group of slavers and into another slaver's clutches. But maybe spaceships simply had a logical layout to them, one that Crux understood. She was hoping that was true, because she didn't have the strength to fight someone who could breathe fire.

Could he breathe it? She'd seen him use his power, but the fire had come from behind her and she hadn't looked to see the source. Maybe it came from his hands.

It didn't matter. He had power over flames, and she had a bludgeon made of roller skates. Not exactly an even match.

Crux ducked into a small room and came back a moment later with two strange wraps that had a sturdy base to them. He handed them to her and turned away.

"What am I supposed to do with these?" She put her hand against the base and wondered if he wanted her to wrap her fingers like they were about to box, but the base held her hand flat, rather than in a fist.

"You said you needed shoes," he responded as if that explained everything.

Courtney took another look. Well. *Maybe* she could make it work. She set the wraps on the ground and stepped onto the base. With a little work she managed to wrap the loose fabric around her ankles and fashion something like a sandal. It was flimsy, and she was sure she was going to fall over. But after she took two or three steps, something strange happened. The material of the base of the sandal warmed up and seemed to mold to her foot, and when she looked down, they didn't look loose at all.

Cool.

Maybe the aliens weren't all bad. This kind of shoe technology blew anything she knew out of the water.

But she was quickly reminded of just how bad the ship was when a scream rent the air. Crux shoved her back into the tiny storage area where he'd found the shoes and joined her, blocking her view of the hallway with his body.

Footsteps hustled, slapping against the metal, and something was dragged behind them. She heard pleading words and gasping cries and wanted to run out and save whoever was in trouble.

Instead she waited. She told herself that Crux would stop her from doing something as stupid as charging straight into the enemy, but he didn't have to do anything to hold her back except stand there. She held herself in place.

A few moments later, the footsteps and cries were gone. She and Crux shared a look, and even though he was an alien dragon, she could read the regret in his expression.

"I'll come back and save who I can," he promised, lips tight and eyes grim.

Courtney nodded. He wasn't promising her, she understood. He was promising himself. He couldn't walk away and leave people to suffer.

Crux made sure the hallway was clear before leading her out and down to another store room. This one was full of strange looking tools. Crux took his time looking them over before choosing one and attempting to remove her collar. It didn't do anything.

He went through five more tools before his shoulders slumped. "The proper keys are likely to be on the guards. We'll need to find one, and I can't char him, as it would risk the tool we need. Stay close. We're almost done."

But maybe luck had turned to their favor. "I bashed a guard's head in when I escaped. Maybe he's still by my cell." She could still remember the sickening crunch. Did it count as murder when it was an alien? That was another thing Courtney couldn't think about too closely.

Crux didn't seem concerned about the morality of alien murder. "Can you find your way back there?"

Courtney nodded. Now that she was back on the ship, she could make sense of where she was. It wasn't nearly as disorienting as her escape had been. But she didn't take the lead. Crux followed her directions as she told him which way to go, but he stayed ahead of her just in case they met any aliens intent on destruction.

They didn't.

They made it to her old cell in just a few minutes, and Courtney was disappointed to see that the alien she had beaten was no longer there. "He looked dead when I left," she said, preemptively defending herself.

But Crux didn't want to hold it against her. "His compatriots might have moved his corpse. Or, perhaps, you merely rendered him unconscious. It doesn't matter. Let's scavenge some food and find a place to hide for the night. I don't want to get caught out after sundown."

"Any particular reason?" She tried not to focus on the way the collar hung heavily around her throat. She wanted it off. Now. But that wasn't going to happen yet.

"I find it's best not to be caught out on a strange planet in the dark, not until I can find out what dangers lurk." He led her down another hallway.

Dangers. Great. And he wasn't talking about the

alien slavers. She didn't want to think about the scary shit that might be haunting the planet.

Crux found a machine and activated the screen, pressing buttons as they lit up. A few moments later, a small hatch beside the screen opened and revealed a stack of what looked like individually wrapped granola bars and four canteens.

Her protector looked her up and down before grabbing all of the food and stuffing it in his own pockets. Probably for the best. Courtney didn't have pockets of her own. And she hated to think how something would taste if she stuck it in her skate boot to carry it.

They were lucky not to meet any more aliens as they escaped the ship and Crux led them back into the forest. He moved with the kind of surety that made her wonder if he'd been here before today. Then she realized he was looking at some sort of tablet on his wrist.

"What's that?" she asked. Her mouth was dry, and she could really use some water. She hoped they could stop soon.

"I released a dragonet when I arrived. It's mapping the planet and sending me information." He turned suddenly and they headed up hill.

"There's a baby dragon out there?" This planet was no place for a baby, even if it was a dragon.

Crux laughed. "That must be a translation error.

No. The dragonet is a small machine that flies and relays information back to me. All the baby dragons are safe at home, I should hope."

"Oh, so it's a drone." That she understood.

But Crux might not have heard her. They stood at the mouth of a small cave. "Wait here," he instructed before plunging inside.

She felt highly exposed, but there were no evil aliens around to nab her. She was safe. She just had to keep telling herself that.

A moment later, Crux came out. "There doesn't appear to be anything living in the cave. Should be safe enough for the night."

A cave. Wonderful. Courtney wouldn't call herself a camper, but just like with everything else, she didn't have another choice. She entered the cave.

At first it was pitch black, but Crux got a fire started quickly and arranged a small sitting space for her. It wasn't comfortable. They didn't have blankets or pillows. But it was better than nothing.

He set something up by the entrance to the cave.

"What's that?" For a moment, something shivered in front of the cave's opening, but then Courtney blinked and it looked normal again.

"A small force field generator. It will keep anything outside from coming in. I don't want any surprises during the night."

"Good call." She didn't want to imagine what kind

of scary creatures might be waiting for them outside. And she certainly didn't want to be caught off guard by any of the alien slavers.

They settled in, and a short time later, Crux offered her the granola bar and a canteen. Courtney tore into the meal, not caring how it tasted. The light slowly started to dim outside and she was grateful for the fire.

Then the sun set completely.

For a moment, it was peaceful. Then she heard the rabid cry of an animal in distress. Then another. Then it was like a hundred beasts howling in unison.

Something thumped against the force field, but after a moment, it seemed to hold.

"What's out there?" she whispered, afraid to summon the monsters with the sound of her voice. The crackle of the fire was loud enough to make her worry.

Crux was grim again. "I don't know. But it sounds like we must be sure not to be caught out after sundown."

The monsters kept screaming, and Courtney knew she wouldn't sleep.

6

AFTER ABOUT AN HOUR, the worst of the screams and howls seemed to quiet, or maybe Courtney just got used to them. Crux gave her two more granola bars, and she finished off all the liquid in her canteen. It was thicker than water, sweeter too, but not unpleasant to drink. She didn't ask what it was. She'd had enough surprises for one day.

Crux was sitting a polite distance away, and for some reason, that made her antsy. She looked at the entrance to the cave and saw something fly quickly in front of it, one dark speck moving across the dark sky, almost impossible to perceive. And the only thing protecting them from it was an invisible piece of technology she didn't understand.

That was one thing she could fix. "How does it work?"

Crux looked up from where he'd been staring at the fire and tilted his head in confusion. "What?"

"How does the force field thing work?" She wasn't science minded, but she needed to have some idea of what was going on.

Crux blinked a few times and grimaced. "I regret to say I'm not exactly sure. Something about exciting the molecules within range to solidify them and prevent unwanted intrusions. I promise it works, we've been using them for years."

Courtney slumped against the wall and pulled her legs up to hold them close. Her skates were sitting at her side, in reach if she found herself in need of a weapon but not adding unwanted weight to her shoulders anymore. "So you find yourself holed up in caves hiding from monsters a lot?"

He gave a comforting smile. "Less often than you'd think. We use a modified version of the force field device back home to seal up the windows in buildings to prevent theft and nasty bugs from getting inside. Also works for heat and cold if you adjust the settings correctly, but still can let in breezes. The technology has been around for centuries."

She blew out a breath at that thought. "Centuries. Damn. Sounds like you're pretty advanced."

"Advanced?" He sounded puzzled and shifted a little closer to her, probably to hear better over the crackling fire. "What do you mean? That makes it sound like there's some sort of predetermined path for civilization."

"Isn't there?" Courtney tried to imagine it based on what she'd been taught. "There's pre-history, you know, people hiding out in caves while monsters stalk outside." They shared a smile at that. "Then people learn to farm. There's kingdoms and cities. Eventually someone discovers electricity. There's space travel. I don't know. Seems like a predetermined path to me."

Crux didn't immediately respond, and the thoughtful look on his face made her wonder if she'd said something wrong. "And no society ever deviates? None ever regresses? There is only a forward path to progress?"

"Well, when you say it like that, clearly not." She hugged her knees even tighter. "But it's comforting to think that there's a road laid out ahead."

"Yes, I imagine it is." He didn't even sound smug when he said it, the asshole.

He looked even better in firelight. He was back in his regular human form, but he still wore the utilitarian clothing he'd appeared in when he'd rescued her. It was all back, sleeves pulled up to reveal very nice forearms, and muscles that weren't hidden under all that fabric. His face was sharp and shadowed, the fire making it shift as the flames crackled.

She would have never known he was an alien if she'd seen him on Earth. She probably wouldn't have been able to untie her tongue to talk to him either. He wasn't just hot, he was intimidatingly attractive. Almost insultingly attractive. It actually annoyed her how beautiful he was. And competent. And fire breathing.

"Have I done something wrong?" Crux asked out of nowhere.

"What?" Courtney shook herself out of her train of thought.

"You were scowling at me like I'd asked for favors you refused to permit." He nodded at the fire. "Would you like me to move to the other side?"

"You're fine. And so am I. It wasn't about you." Well, it totally was, but she wasn't going to admit that his hotness bordered on offensive. "What's your home like? Are you really a prince?" It was harder to believe that he was a prince than it was to accept he was a dragon.

"My father is King Venin, the Dragon King, and I am his oldest son. That makes me a prince. One day I will be the Dragon King. Though I hope not for a long time." He shuddered. "Despite our differences, I do love my father and have no wish to see him ill.

Nor do I have any wish to shoulder his responsibilities yet."

Dragon King. Cool. Cool cool cool. Courtney bit her tongue to keep from saying anything about that.

"I live in the palace at Dragon City. It's a small city, perhaps thirty-thousand people all told. Hardly the biggest in the kingdom, but more than acceptable for my brothers and I. I fear we might make life difficult if we lived in one of the larger cities. We've found the kingdom functions better when the royal family lives at some remove from everyone."

"We had out of touch royals once too. It didn't end well." She only realized what she'd said once she said it, and her eyes got wide and she pressed her lips together tightly to keep from saying anything else.

But it only made Crux laugh. "My father has residences in every major city in the kingdom and several in smaller towns. He rotates his living quarters every other year and tours the country—at his own expense—with some frequency. I am not so blind that I'd call him perfect, but he does know his people."

"And do you?" She was American enough not to like the idea of a king with unlimited power, but also American enough to be fascinated by royalty.

"I have, but for now I am more focused on honing my warrior skills."

"Is that what brought you here?" She was

thankful, but it did seem strange. As far as she knew, he had no connection to this planet or anyone who was on that ship. If it was random chance that had rescued her, she'd be thankful, but she needed to know.

That brough Crux up short, and he stared back at the fire for several moments. "I came here for my own reasons. My father has… it doesn't matter. I am glad that I could be of service to you. I despise slavers and will stop them wherever I can."

It wasn't an answer, but Courtney got the idea that he wouldn't answer if she pressed. And she wasn't entitled to his truth, no matter how much she wanted to know.

"It's late," he said. "You should sleep."

"I don't think that's likely." She could feel exhaustion pressing down on her, but the thought of actually closing her eyes made her want to break out in hives.

"I'll keep you safe," he promised. "And I'll stay far away. No need to worry about me."

She hadn't worried about that at all. "Actually." She hated to ask. He'd already done so much for her. But she had one idea of how she might make sleep come. "Do you think you could sleep close? Right next to me. I'm… feeling kind of alone right now. You don't have to say yes," she was quick to add. "You've already done a lot."

But Crux just scooted closer and laid down between her and the entrance to the cave. Courtney laid down, careful not to touch him, but comforted by the warmth of his body.

She wanted to ask him to hold her and tell her everything would be okay, but she couldn't make the words come out. She told herself it would be okay and hoped that eventually she could manage to sleep.

Then Crux's arm came over her side and she smiled.

7

CRUX KNEW he shouldn't enjoy the warm body pressed up against him as much as he did. She wasn't his mate. She wasn't his anything.

No, that wasn't quite right.

For now, she was his responsibility. He had to get her off this planet and to safety. Anything else would be reprehensible. But that wasn't why he was here. The matchmaker had told him that his mate would be waiting for him.

Had he been tricked?

Many things were said about the matchmaker. But he'd never heard any word of her being malicious.

Courtney shifted as she fell deeper into her slumber, and her body brushed against his. Crux had to bite back a moan and shift away to keep her from feeling the effect she had on him. She was so deeply asleep that it might not register, but he was unwilling to take the risk.

She wouldn't want him, and he couldn't have her.

A small, ironic laugh escaped at that thought. He was a dragon prince. Almost everything in the kingdom was his for the taking. And yet he was reduced to lustful sleep in a cave because the woman in his arms was not his.

The conniving part of his mind tried to convince him that he could take her, provided she was willing. His mate was nowhere to be found. He had made no vows. For all he knew, she was a fantasy dreamed up by a false psychic matchmaker.

But he wouldn't.

Courtney was in no position to take a lover, not with a slave collar around her neck and stolen shoes on her feet. She wanted nothing to do with him.

And under other circumstances, he might have said the same about her. She wasn't a refined lady who knew how to play the seductive games of the dragon aristocracy. She wasn't a warrior who was up for a bit of bed sport with no promises. She was human.

He'd never fucked a human before.

His cock plumped up at the thought.

Crux grit his teeth and tried to think of anything but what the curvy woman in his arms would look like if she was stripped bare. Unfortunately, his mind was only able to focus on exactly what he wasn't supposed to think about.

Curse it.

If it didn't have the potential to send his human screaming, Crux would stroke himself to relief right there. She was deeply in sleep and would never have to know. But if she woke…

No, it wasn't worth the risk.

Damn it all.

He couldn't touch the woman in his arms. He couldn't touch himself. And he had no idea where his real mate was. Instead, Crux turned his mind over to the slavers who had crash landed. They would feel the lick of his fire and edge of his claws.

A cry from outside broke through the force field, and Crux grinned cruelly. That was, if they survived the night.

If he had to bet, he'd say that most of them would. Slavers were a lot devoted to stubborn survival. The ship was probably intact enough to reinforce and defend against the planet's monsters. And if it was, whatever captives were left had a chance at survival.

For that reason and his blood lust, Crux hoped the slavers survived. For now.

Courtney shifted again and let out a little sigh, and all of Crux's martial thought flew out the hatch as his cock surged back to life.

He reached down and pressed a hand firmly against his trousers, as if that would somehow make his offending organ behave.

It only served to incite him.

He rolled away from Courtney. The temptation of her skin was too much for him to handle. He sprang to his feet and checked the force field, since he had nothing else to do. It was holding nicely and he had no worries about it lasting until morning.

That only took a minute, and his cock was still hard as stone.

He looked at the sleeping Courtney and wondered what it was about her that made his body react like a man with no discipline. He'd been in much more tempting situations and hadn't flinched from his duty. There was nothing tempting about this, and now he found his hand creeping to his cock again.

Stress?

His father's dictate?

The fact that his freedom was being torn away?

Or was there something special about the human woman dozing on the dirt?

Thinking about it only made it worse. Rather than spend the night staring at the object of his desire, Crux explored the cave. It wasn't much to look at. From the disturbed pile of leaves and branches in one corner, he imagined something had made a nest in here at one point, but whatever had, it was long gone.

He turned a corner and found a pool.

Crux grinned.

He wanted to dive right in, but his survival instincts were stronger than that. He went back to the fire where he'd laid down his small survival pack and pulled out a scanner. A quick scan of the water showed it was safe to drink and use, though the temperature reading made him shudder at the thought of the cold.

Just what he needed.

He stripped off his clothes and settled in, wincing as the icy chill settled into his bones. He was a dragon, made for fire and heat, not ice. But the shock of the water was enough to calm his body down.

Crux submerged himself completely and stayed in the icy water until his teeth started to chatter. Once he was done, he pulled himself out of the pool and summoned his warrior form, letting out some of his own fire to warm his body and dry him off.

He was careful not to look at Courtney. Thinking of her would make the whole exercise pointless.

He put his clothes back on and sat by the fire, within reach of the woman but not close enough to touch. That way lay a danger he wasn't ready to face.

He needed a plan. It was a necessity of any battle,

and that was what this excursion was. So Crux planned.

Step one: remove Courtney's collar and send her to his people.

Step two: kill the slavers and free their captives.

Step three: find his mate.

Simple. So simple it only took him a minute to think it.

The sky was still dark, and if it weren't for the predators, he might risk a longer walk to think things through. He was missing something. Something that he knew was important. But the day had been long and Crux was not a god. He needed his rest too.

He looked at Courtney for a long while before settling down several feet away from her. He would not allow himself to give into that temptation. He was a man of discipline, even if his fingers ached to feel her hair.

Think of your mate, he implored his mind. But that was a blank. The matchmaker had told him nothing of his mate, other than the fact that she was *here.* If it was a trap, it was finely sprung.

But he believed the matchmaker. His mate was somewhere on this planet and he was going to find her.

He just had to put Courtney out of his mind.

8

Courtney splashed water on her face to try and clear the sleep from her body. Crux had shaken her shoulder to wake her up just as dawn broke outside, and she was shocked at how well she had slept.

Maybe knowing a dragon was keeping her safe was enough to keep the nightmares at bay.

She splashed herself again, not particularly caring if she got her clothes wet. Besides, the collar was blocking most of the water from hitting her shirt. That was one good thing about it.

Cold water in the face wasn't as good as coffee, but it was all she had. She took one of the granola bars once she was done cleaning and scarfed it down. They were surprisingly filling for something that tasted like old cardboard, but she'd much rather have an omelet.

"What's the plan?" she asked as Crux doused their fire. It filled the area with smoke that made her eyes water until he breathed deep and sucked up all the smoke, reminding her he wasn't as human as he looked. "Neat trick."

Crux gave her a polite smile. There was a distance to him today that hadn't been there last night, and Courtney tried to think of what she'd done to cause it. But unless she'd said something terrible in her sleep, she couldn't think of anything.

Oh god, had she said something terrible in her sleep?

She was saved the embarrassment of asking when Crux spoke. "We're going to get that collar off you and get you out of here. Hopefully your nightmare will be over in just a few hours."

He sounded optimistic, and Courtney wanted to believe him. But her cynicism ran deep, and nothing so far had gone the way it was supposed to. "I'm ready when you are," she said with false confidence.

She didn't know if Crux believed her or not, but they set out anyway. She didn't see any sign of the monsters that they'd heard the night before and wondered for a while if she'd imagined them. Then they made it a little further down the hill and passed by the bones of a creature that hadn't been there the day before.

"Did those monsters do that?" she asked, trying

not to imagine what it would feel like to have her flesh ripped from her bones. There wasn't even a speck of blood left.

"Most likely," he confirmed. "We're safe as long as we have cover," he tried to comfort her.

It wasn't much comfort.

They continued on and Courtney's collar chafed. She stuck her fingers under the metal and tried to pull it away from her skin for a bit of relief, but it didn't loosen. When that didn't work, she rolled her head around, trying to stretch her neck. That didn't do much either, and she stopped bothering. Crux was going to find the tool he needed to remove the collar and get her to safety.

She hoped she was right to put her trust in him.

They passed another pile of bones, this one with a skeletal structure that was almost, but not quite, human. "Is that one of the aliens that took me?"

Crux studied the bones. "It appears so. Don't waste your pity on him. He died too quick."

"No pity here." She didn't care how fast or slow that thing had died. She just wanted to be away from them.

As they got closer to the remains of the ship, Crux moved with more care, and Courtney became insanely aware of every step she took. Every leaf that crunched under her feet was a potential alarm for the surviving aliens.

She hoped the monsters had thinned the herd.

Crux had shifted to look more alien with those faint scales and claws, and the promise of fire. Compared to that, her roller skates didn't feel like much, but they were still slung over her shoulders and ready to bash in any alien heads that got too close.

As they got closer to the ship, she found herself wondering about where exactly Crux was sending her. It was too dangerous to ask now, and she realized that she'd wasted her opportunity the night before. He'd told her a little, but she wasn't prepared.

She trusted him. She didn't want to get sent to some other random planet far from home.

But hopefully there wouldn't be monsters there.

Did dragons count as monsters?

Well, maybe the bad ones. But she seemed to have a good dragon on her side.

"Stay close, we don't want them snatching you," he warned.

No, no they did not.

She didn't hear any screams this morning, but didn't know if that was good or bad. Screams meant survivors. But they also meant fear. She hoped whoever was still trapped on the ship was merely exhausted and nothing worse.

Footsteps echoed around them as they snuck onto the ship and hid in an out of the way corridor. The alien slaver that crossed their path didn't know what hit him as Crux launched himself at him with a speed that made him blur in front of Courtney's eyes.

She thanked any deity that was listening that he was on her side.

He lowered the dead alien quietly to the floor and rifled through his pockets with scary efficiency. He came up with a small electronic device and studied it for a moment.

"This should do the trick." He pointed it at her and pressed a button.

Courtney flinched, expecting pain. But all that happened was that the clasp of the collar came undone and it fell off her neck. She caught it at the last minute and then had to quickly rebalance to keep her skates from slipping off her shoulder.

Crux shot her a look that was half amused, half impressed.

Courtney glared.

Then she rolled her neck and enjoyed the sweet freedom of movement. She didn't know if she'd ever be able to even wear a necklace again. She didn't want to be reminded of what it felt like to have all that metal around her throat. No, thank you.

Crux stowed the remote away in one of his many pockets and then pulled out his teleportation device.

"Thanks for saving my life," she said before she lost the chance. "Will I ever see you again?" She couldn't help but feel like she was missing out on something right now, like there was something she was supposed to do.

But that was probably just the trauma talking.

"I'm sure I won't be far behind you," he promised. "You'll see me before you return home." He pressed a button on the teleporter.

The day before, the portal had opened immediately, a scar of white light on the fabric of reality.

Today nothing happened.

He pressed the button again.

Still nothing.

"Is it out of battery?" Courtney asked, though the idea that some sort of practically magical teleporter ran on batteries was ludicrous.

"Of course not," Crux bit out. Then he shook it and hit it against his palm just like a television remote that was running out of juice. He hit the button again.

Nothing.

"Damn it all." He raised his fist high in the air, ready to toss it away, but seemed to think better at the last moment and lowered his hand to glare at the device. "It appears the device is malfunctioning. Something must have been knocked loose while I fought. Don't worry. There will be something that can fix it on board the ship."

Would there?

Courtney's heart sank. Sure, she hadn't wanted to leave Crux behind and travel to an unknown planet, but now that she had no choice but to stay, she found herself almost desperate to step through the portal to safety.

But there was no such thing as safety. Not on this planet. Probably not where he was from, and certainly not back home. She had no choice but to soldier on and survive.

"Okay, let's go find the parts." If they kept moving, she wouldn't have to think about how terrified she was.

Crux looked ready to say something, but more footsteps echoed down the hall. "Is there something we could use to cover him up?" He nodded at the body on the floor. "I'd rather he wasn't immediately discovered."

Good point.

They found a large storage trunk that was only half full and it took both of them to manage to stash the corpse away. Courtney tried not to think too closely about what she was doing.

She just had to survive a little longer.

She didn't have another choice.

9

Crux tried not to let the frustration get to him. A broken teleporter was entirely fixable. And, if not, he could always send a message for help. But he hated to be a failure, and he didn't want to risk Courtney.

"Let's find you some place to hide," he said once the slaver's body was stowed away. He'd start to smell soon enough, but they'd be long gone before he was discovered.

"Hide?" It came out loud enough that Crux glared at the human and strained his ears to make sure no slavers were coming.

"Of course. You'll hide, I'll find the parts I need, then I'll send you to Dragon City where you can rest until I send you home. That's the plan." Why were they wasting time reiterating it?

"I thought we established that hiding me just

makes it more likely that the slavers will find me and *enslave* me again. No, thank you." She shook her head violently, one of her wheeled shoes bouncing against her chest as she moved.

But he wasn't looking at her chest.

"That was when I thought we'd only be here a matter of minutes. Please, be reasonable." He needed to be rid of this woman as soon as he could. She played havoc on his mind and made him forget his mission.

"Reasonable? I've been so much more than reasonable. Have I complained? Have I argued? No. Come on, Crux."

He didn't need to think about how good his name sounded on her lips. "You're arguing now." His mate wouldn't argue, that he was certain of.

"Because you're being stupid. Let's go get this part, then you can send me off to god knows where and you can do whatever it is you're here to do. Why are we waiting?" She nodded down the hall and leaned forward, as if she were ready to walk off, but when he didn't move, she stayed still.

"You put every captive on this ship at risk by arguing with me. Especially my—" he cut himself off.

But Courtney heard him anyway. "Your what? Why are you really here? It's not random, is it?"

He could lie. He could tell her only half the truth. He didn't owe her anything. But lies withered on his tongue. "I came through the portal to find my fated mate. I have reason to believe she's on this planet."

Courtney blinked a few times in surprise. "Sure. Why not? If dragons exist, mates are a thing too. Do you have any other bombshells you want to drop?"

"You mock me." A mate was a gift like no other, something Crux had thought impossible for himself. And Courtney reacted like he was speaking nonsense. His inner fire surged within him, lighting his blood as he seethed.

Her eyes got wide and she took a step back, but there was a wall in place to keep her from moving very far. "You're smoking."

Crux looked down and saw she was right. Smoke rose from his skin, a lack of control that only happened to the youngest or most emotionally unstable dragons. He doused his inner fire, calling it back to the core of himself, and the steam dissipated. "Let's find you somewhere to hide."

"I'd really rather be next to the guy who breathes fire rather than hiding in a closet somewhere." She wasn't going to be put aside easily.

And when she put it that way, Crux understood her point a bit better, but she spoke before he could say anything.

"No wonder you want to hide me away, if your girlfriend is out there somewhere. You wouldn't want to make her jealous." Then she huffed out a derisive laugh. "Not that she'd be jealous of me."

Crux stopped short and looked Courtney up and down. "You think you could not spark jealousy in someone?" With his blood already hot, he remembered what she looked like while she lay down, and it was nothing to imagine her stripped bare. If his true mate knew his thoughts, she would have every right to be jealous.

But Courtney could not read his mind and shrugged with a wry twist of her lips. "I'm not... it doesn't matter. Can we go now and find the parts before the aliens attack us?"

She wasn't going to give up, that was clear. And he could keep arguing or take her with him.

Arguing was wasting time.

It was echoing footsteps that decided him. "Come on." He led her further into the ship. He didn't know the exact schematics, but the design was intuitive enough, and Crux had no issue finding the mechanic's quarters. It was just as full of goodies as he hoped.

"Keep watch," he said as he headed deeper into the room, which was little bigger than a closet.

Courtney stroked the wheeled shoe hanging over her shoulder with a nod. A few minutes later, she spoke. "Why can you use a teleporter and these guys need a ship?"

Crux dug through a box of tiny screws before putting it aside to examine a spool of wire. Courtney's question was a reminder of just how backwards her planet was. Any child back home could answer it. "Teleporters are expensive and they can only transfer matter over short distance. And the amount of matter is fairly limited."

"How short are we talking?" She leaned out into the hall, taking her watch duty seriously.

Crux didn't tell her that if the slavers were in sight, they were already too close. They'd hear them coming long before they saw them. "About a billion miles with four to five people."

"Oh, only a billion." It was good to know that her translator was advanced enough to handle sarcasm.

"It's closer than you think." He'd been thinking in galactic terms since he was a child, even though his kingdom was confined to one planet. It was a peaceful planet and the best way to get warrior training was to journey into space. "A billion miles doesn't even reach the edge of the solar system."

Courtney sucked in a breath. "Jesus Christ, I'm in space." She slumped against the door jamb, and he had a feeling that if she wasn't supposed to be keeping watch, she would have slid to the floor in defeat.

Crux pocketed a few more items and a tool he'd need to solder everything together. He hated to take a chance with a wonky teleporter, but if he couldn't get communications through, it might be his only shot at safety. "Let's get out of here."

"Don't you need to rescue your mate?" There was something in her tone that he couldn't read.

Did she have a point? Crux had left the rest of the captured women on the ship on the theory he'd be able to quickly teleport Courtney away and then deal with them. Now he didn't know how long it would take and what tortures they would endure in his absence.

His mate was supposed to be out there somewhere. It didn't feel real. Even if it sounded like a childish fancy, he'd thought he'd be able to sense her somehow. But the only person he was paying any attention to was Courtney.

"I need a plan before I come back to rescue them," he finally said. He hoped his mate would forgive him one day. "Let's move."

They'd barely stepped into the hallway when heavy footsteps started moving their way fast.

Crux grabbed Courtney and dragged her back into the mechanic's closet.

10

C OURTNEY'S HEART pounded hard as the slavers' boots stomped in the hallway on the other side of the door. She was supremely aware of just how close they were to the alien slaver that they'd killed and that the door wasn't that thick.

If they made noise, they'd be heard.

Was her heart too loud? Was her breath? It was coming fast, hyperventilation threatening, and Courtney couldn't calm herself down.

Then Crux wrapped an arm around her midsection and pulled her close against him.

It shouldn't have been comforting. They were trapped in a closet together on the edge of discovery. He was probably mad at her since she wouldn't hide like a good little woman.

And he had a mate.

Why did that disappoint her?

It was difficult to wrap her head around at all. Mate? Seriously? That sounded like something out of a movie. *Mars Needs Mates!* But they weren't on Mars, and he was dead serious. One of the other women who'd been captured was his destined girlfriend.

He'd only helped Courtney because she was there. He was only holding her to keep her from doing something stupid.

He. Had. A. Mate.

So why did her body want to melt back against his and feel if he was really hard all over? It had to be a response to all the trauma. He was her only constant, her only bit of safety, so of course she wanted to cling to him in all ways possible.

It didn't even have anything to do with Crux. It could have been anyone.

Even as she thought it, she was pretty sure that was a bunch of bullshit.

Crux shifted his grip, and his hand flattened against her stomach. Her breath fluttered, and she closed her eyes, trying to block out the sensation. He wasn't even touching her anywhere *good*. His thumb was inches from her breast, and he'd have to move his whole hand if he were going to cup it and stroke her nipple to hardness.

She bit her lip as she imagined it, her body lighting up at the thought.

She held herself as still as she could, pushing away all sensation. But in the dark of the closet, with the feel of Crux all around her, that was impossible.

Then his lips brushed over her ear, and Courtney was *not* responsible for the small gasp that escaped. No way.

"You're doing good," he whispered, his breath tickling her, his voice low.

She could imagine him saying something like that in another situation, both of them stripped bare while he pushed into her deep and coaxed an unknowable pleasure out of her. He'd be good at sex. Amazing at it. And she'd never imagined fucking a prince, not as any sort of real possibility.

But this one she wanted.

He didn't move his head away from the crook of her neck, and Courtney found herself leaning back into him. She knew she shouldn't, but madness had overtaken her, and there was nothing that could make her stop, not even if the slavers outside busted down the door.

That should have been a warning.

It wasn't.

Crux's lips brushed against her ear again, but this time he didn't say anything. She tilted her head and he took the hint, lips brushing down her neck in featherlight kisses.

He had a mate. This was wrong.

But it felt so right.

Courtney wasn't a cheater. She didn't date more than one guy at a time. And she hadn't dated anyone in a while after the last disaster.

But this wasn't cheating, her body insisted. Crux hadn't met his mate. And they were doing nothing wrong.

His hand moved higher, and his thumb brushed over her nipple.

Her lip was going to be bruised from how hard she was biting it to keep from making a noise.

She moved her hips and was shocked to feel the rock hard length behind her. She wasn't the only one who wanted this, who wanted more. And as Crux brushed his fingers against her, she was possessed by some kind of demonic lust that made her rub her hips against him until he hissed out a pleasured groan.

She thought she smelled smoke, and when she breathed deeper, she was sure of it. Crux was smoking again, and this time she could feel the heat of his skin as he sizzled.

"You undo me," he whispered in her ear, the words a secret that belonged to the dark.

"More." She wanted whatever he could give her. When they stepped out of this closet, she had no doubt they'd pretend this moment had ever happened, so Courtney wanted everything he was willing to give right now. So far, her journey to outer space had sucked. She wanted one good thing out of it.

For a moment, she thought she'd asked for too much when Crux pulled his hand away. But he only moved it down far enough to hike up her shirt and get his fingers on her naked skin.

Yes.

That was it. If his fingers over her shirt were a temptation, then his fingers on her flesh were almost more than she could bear. She jerked her hips back and felt him thrust against her, his own desire starting to override his good sense.

How would he look if she dropped to her knees in front of him?

What would she do if *he* dropped to *his* knees?

She'd lose it. She was already wet and desperate for more. And if Crux was on his knees in front of her and looking up at her with wicked intent, she wouldn't be able to control what she did next.

He pinched her nipple just hard enough to make Courtney hiss. Her other breast felt neglected, but she couldn't complain from the expert way he was touching her. He knew exactly where to stroke, where to kiss. And they weren't even unclothed.

He was sex incarnate and a real danger to her. But nothing could make Courtney back away. There was room for her to step forward, to break the contact between them. She could put an end to this at any moment.

But she wasn't going to. This was her break from sanity. Her break from the horror that waited in the hall outside. Crux could give her this much.

And she took it like it was her due.

She reached behind her and ran her fingers over the hard length of his cock. It felt normal enough, but she wondered if a dragon would be any different than a human man. She wanted to find out.

She'd never heard a human man make such an animalistic sound as she stroked him. She couldn't get a good grip on Crux, not at this angle, but she didn't want to stop him from touching her.

Crux grabbed her wrist and stopped her from doing more. If he could see her, she'd be ashamed of the way she pouted. And she hated the sound she made when he pulled his hand out of her shirt and stopped touching her.

He put inches between them, and she felt more alone than she had in a long time.

Silence hung heavy in the darkness around them. Courtney's body was flushed with desire, and she wanted Crux to quench it. She was tempted to spin around and see if he could resist her if he had to look her in the face.

But she couldn't face the rejection, and a slamming door somewhere deep in the ship reminded her of just how much trouble they were teetering on the edge of.

"We need to get out of here," Crux said, voice gravelly and gruff.

Courtney didn't hear any aliens outside, but she was pretty sure they weren't leaving because the coast was clear. Crux didn't want the temptation of the dark.

And she had to remember that he had a mate waiting for him somewhere. He wasn't hers to keep.

11

IF CRUX THOUGHT his hard cock from the night before was bad, it had nothing on what he walked through danger with today. The weight of Courtney's breast was imprinted on his hand, and he'd remember the way she bit back those noises for the rest of his life.

It should have felt like a betrayal.

He had no idea why it felt so right.

But he needed to get away from her before he did something unforgiveable, like bend her over the nearest surface and dive into her tight heat until he didn't know where he ended and she began.

His cock surged at the thought, and it was only the reminder that slavers could find them at any moment that kept him under the slightest modicum of control.

His human—Courtney, not *his* anything—was breathing heavily, and he was sure if he'd been brave enough to delve a hand into those leggings of hers, he would have found her wet. She'd been pliant against him, eager for the pleasures of the flesh, and he wanted to lose himself in her.

He was on a mission. A mission that didn't include her. Bloodlust had a way of sparking the other kind of lust, and Crux tried to convince himself that this was all that was. He was eager for battle, and when he couldn't fight, he'd take another kind of contact.

But he could not fool himself. He wanted Courtney, and it had nothing to do with fighting.

He led her off the ship and she followed quietly. There was no argument now, but he knew he'd hear her mind when they got back to their cave. This whole day had been a failure of epic proportions. Once they were outside, Crux turned his head toward the sky to judge the star's position in the sky.

Days were short here and nights long. They only had a few hours left before they needed to return to the safety of the cave.

And if he could not get the teleporter fixed, he'd call for help in the morning. He needed to get Courtney to safety and send the temptation away.

They both froze when they heard a feminine

scream, and there was no need for communication to head towards it.

Crux took the lead, and he was sure Courtney had a firm hold on her improvised weapon.

A group of slavers stood in a half circle, corralling their enslaved cargo. And just to the side of one of the slavers was a rent in the air that signaled a portal. They had a functioning teleporter.

"I thought you said teleporters only work over short," Courtney gave a faint snort at that word, "distances." She edged up closer to them. "So what's that?"

"They must have a ship nearby. If we get their teleporter, I can reprogram it." He studied the group. He doubted the frightened women would be a danger to him, especially if they saw Courtney working with him. From this distance, all the women appeared to be humans like Courtney, but he couldn't be sure. From a distance, someone might think he was human too.

The slavers would be a problem. There were four of them. Normally Crux would use his flame to take care of the problem, but it posed too much of a risk both to the women he wanted to rescue and the teleporter he needed to escape.

He called on his warrior form and flexed his claws.

It was time to get a bit bloody.

"Don't let them throw you through the portal," he warned.

"Thanks, Captain Obvious," she scoffed. "What else should I do?"

She wasn't a warrior, but she was brave, and he could use that. He wanted to keep her safe, but it was an impossible task at the moment. Crux gave it a bit of consideration. "If I lure the slavers away, try to get the women to run. Lead them back to the cave we slept in, and I'll follow shortly after." He reached into his pocket and pulled out the force field generator. "Seal off the entrance. I can signal you if I make it back before nightfall."

She took the generator and studied it for a minute. "You will make it back, right?"

It was four on one. Crux was good, but even he couldn't predict based on that. "I'll do my best."

She stuck the generator in a pocket and then grabbed his arm to hold him in place. "You have to come back. You're the one getting the teleporter." Her tone was deceptively light.

In any other circumstance, Crux might have kissed her for luck. He could imagine what her lips would taste like. He'd already stolen a taste of her skin. But those thoughts had no place on the battlefield.

No place in his mind at all.

"I'll come back." He shouldn't have promised, but

he could do nothing else. "Wait here until you have your moment."

She nodded and clutched her wheeled shoe.

Crux left her, trusting her to follow his order. He got as close as he could without alerting anyone and let his fire blow out of him, aiming not for the slavers and their victims but for trees on the other side of the clearing. He didn't want to attack his enemy, he wanted them distracted.

It worked.

For two of the slavers.

They jerked up and started panicking, talking over each other and pointing wildly. The other two were much more disciplined. One picked up a blaster and looked around with the cool eyes of an experienced soldier while the other stepped closer to the prisoners to keep them from running.

Crux had been afraid of that. He hoped Courtney figured out to run back to the cave by herself if she couldn't get to the women.

Even as he thought it, he knew she wouldn't. She'd rescue them or die trying.

His heart clenched. There was no way he would let her die while he was breathing.

One of the panicking soldiers stepped back, fleeing the fire or his companions, and he backed right into Crux's hiding place. One swipe of Crux's claws had the man falling to the forest floor dead.

One down, three to go.

The light faded fast as night came on, and in the distance, Crux heard the terrifying cry of one of the monsters who hunted on this planet. The remaining slavers heard it too. The portal closed and a slaver stuck the device in his pocket. He said something to his two companions and they corralled the prisoners into a huddle between them and headed back towards the ship.

Crux could give chase, but he didn't know when the planet's monsters would come out, and he couldn't risk Courtney.

He found her just here he'd left her.

"No luck?" she asked.

"I killed one. The others fled." Failure hang heavy on his shoulders, but he tried to push it aside. "We need to seek shelter for the night."

"Won't they just teleport away?" She sounded ready to charge after the slavers, and Crux wanted to join her.

Instead, he let logic win. "The teleporter gives off a signal that is likely to attract this planet's beasts. That may be why we just heard one cry. If they're smart, they will wait until morning to try again." He hoped. All those lives depended on it.

Courtney looked ready to say something else, but she just nodded and followed him as he headed back to the cave where they would once again sleep for the night.

They only made it a few steps up the hill to the cave when Crux heard the tell-tale sound of slavers' voices. Two more steps saw a group of them huddled outside his and Courtney's cave.

In the distance, another monster screamed.

WHEN COURTNEY SAW the alien slavers outside their cave, she knew they were screwed. Monsters were going to eat them as soon as the sun set, or the slavers would capture them and probably kill them.

They'd definitely kill Crux. Maybe they'd lock her back up.

She would die first.

Crux ran, and she followed. Now was not the time to argue about strategy. The dragon man knew more than her and she had to trust him.

Now would be a really good time to magically manifest dragon powers, but it wasn't going to happen.

"There." Crux pointed further up the hill. The cave was difficult to see, just a dark dot against a dark hill, but Courtney made it out. "We can hide there."

"What if they see us?" They'd have to cross near the path that led to the original cave, and she didn't think she was up to fighting half a dozen slavers.

"As long as we make it to the cave first, we're fine. It only takes a couple of seconds to put up the force field. You still have the generator, right?"

Courtney placed a hand over her pocket and confirmed by touch that the device was there. "I do."

He nodded. "Good. We run together. If they spot us, run ahead of me and set it up, but don't power it on. Once you're in the cave, I'll follow."

"And what if there are monsters in the cave?" She didn't want to catastrophize, but was pretty sure it wasn't catastrophizing when they really were on Monster Planet.

Crux made a series of strange expressions and tilted his head toward the side as he considered it. "We'll just have to hope for luck. We're running out of time."

Courtney did not like the sound of that. But it was true. They were running out of time, and they had to move.

Another monster screamed, and it sounded closer.

But it didn't sound like it was coming from any cave on the hill.

"Let's go," she urged. Her muscles were tight, bunched up and ready to sprint, and she'd start shaking if she didn't move soon.

They moved.

Courtney barely breathed as they made their way up the hill, coming dangerously close to the slavers that had stolen their cave. It was a nice cave. Spacious. Homey. It was *her* cave, and if she had time, she would make Crux get rid of anyone who dared steal it from them.

But there wasn't time. Darkness was falling faster than it should have, and she was terrified of what would happen once all the light was gone. She'd seen those bones. She didn't want to be stripped of all her flesh. It seemed a horribly painful way to go.

Her roller skates swung against her shoulder, one of the wheels hitting the same spot on her chest over and over so that she was sure she'd have a bruise. It was worth it if she ended up needing to bash in more alien skulls.

Bash in skulls. Jesus. What had she come to?

"Run for the cave, now," Crux commanded. He didn't raise his voice, but the urgency sent Courtney sprinting even if she didn't see the threat.

But as soon as she was clear of Crux, she understood. He hadn't seen slavers. It was a pack of the planet's monsters right behind them and moving fast. She got an impression of dark gray skin and large, dark eyes. Big limbs. She didn't see claws or teeth, but she was sure the animals had both. They had to, considering the damage that they wrought.

She made it to the mouth of the cave just as Crux let out an unholy burst of fire at the monsters that had made it within feet of him. Courtney wanted to cry out, needed to do something, but she was too far to hit anything with her skate and he didn't need the warning.

Heat churned within her, and she burned hotter than she'd ever felt before. It didn't feel like a fever. It didn't feel like herself. She didn't know what it was. Battle rage? Fury? She didn't have time to ponder.

She skidded to a stop in front of the mouth of the cave and almost dove into the forbidding darkness of the entrance when two more of the monsters stepped out.

They were flat to the ground and then rose up and up and up until they were as tall as elephants, but lithe like panthers. They were something out a forgotten nightmare, and they opened their mouths to reveal sharpened tusks that could rend her in half in one bite.

The monster closest to her roared, and with that roar come a torrent of saliva and gross monster goo that covered Courtney.

The fire burned even brighter, and she let it out with a scream.

Fire burst out of her mouth and lit the two monsters up. It didn't burn like a regular fire. No, this was like napalm on steroids. In seconds, the monsters burnt to a crisp until only bone remnants were on the ground in front of her.

Crux ran up to her and shepherded her inside of the cave, pulling the generator from her pocket and setting it up with practiced motion. He flicked out a hand and set a pile of debris on fire, giving them light. There were no more monsters in the cave, and the monsters had taken care of any critters that might have lived in there.

With the force field up, she and Crux were safe for now.

But Courtney had no idea what had just happened, what she had just done.

She looked down at her hands, but there was no sign of the fire she'd miraculously summoned. She felt her lips and found them chapped, but her lips ran dry and Monster Planet wasn't doing her any favors.

She looked up at Crux. Maybe it was a trick. Maybe he had done it and she had imagined the whole thing. "How?" It came out scratchy, and her throat was a desert. She needed water and hoped Crux still had one of those canteens somewhere.

He stared at her for several silent seconds before reaching around and retrieving a canteen from his pack. She took it and swallowed the liquid greedily.

It went down hard and she sputtered, hacking half of it back up before trying again.

Finally, she had to put the canteen away. "How?" she asked again. Crux had looked away from her, and he wouldn't look back. She didn't know why, and that made her even more scared than she'd been facing down those two monsters. "How, Crux?" She reached out to put her hand on his arm, but he flinched away from her.

"It's impossible." He said it so quietly that she was sure she wasn't supposed to hear.

"What's impossible?" The fluid was restoring her throat, and she could almost pretend she hadn't actually *breathed fire* if she tried really hard. Of course it was impossible. She was a normal human. Normal humans didn't breathe fire.

"Stay here. Recover. I need to investigate the cave." And before she could stop him, he left her sitting there alone.

13

CRUX KNEW he was the highest level of bastard to leave Courtney sitting barely beyond the force field while he dealt with his own damned emotions. But it was impossible. He was a dragon prince. He would one day be king.

He couldn't have a human mate.

His people, his *father*, had certain expectations. And they would not appreciate if their queen wasn't even from the correct planet. There was no way his father would assent to the match. It didn't matter that fate decreed it. It didn't matter that Courtney had called upon Crux's flame and used it for herself, something that was spoken about in legends because it was that rare.

They would see that she was human and fail to look beyond that, just as he had.

The psychic matchmaker had insisted that he would meet his mate on this journey. In fact, she had told him that the *first* woman he met would be his future, if he could hold onto her.

And he had disregarded that. Because, he had told himself, clearly when she said *woman* she meant *dragon woman*. But it was becoming increasingly clear that there were no dragon females on this planet. There were human women, slavers, and monsters.

And his mate.

Crux scanned the small cave quickly, determining it was safe for the night. There was a little pool of water in this one, too, which he scanned. Clean. And warm to the touch. There must have been a hot spring somewhere.

Courtney would like that.

How could he keep her when this was all done?

How could he walk away?

Crux sat at the edge of the pool and stared into the water as if it would offer him answers. All his saw was his own dim reflection, and he scowled at himself. He was to be king one day, and the decision should have been simple.

He had to do what was best for his people.

But what was that? A loveless marriage to some proper dragon lady? Or one blessed by the hand of fate to the most courageous woman he'd ever met?

Fated pairings did not come along often. His own

father had never found his mate. But Crux had been holding out for thirty years on the hope that he would find his own. And here she was.

Could he really throw her away simply because she wasn't a dragon?

He heard footsteps, but he wasn't ready to talk. From the look Courtney gave him, she wasn't ready to say anything either. He'd acted like such a bastard she must be eager to get away from him.

"Is the water safe?" she asked, hand hovering over the pool.

"Clean and warm," he confirmed.

"Do you have something I can use as a towel? I need to try and clean monster goo off my clothes." She spoke matter of factly, and Crux had the sinking feeling that whatever emotions had been brewing between them before, he'd smashed them to bits.

He reached into his pack and pulled out a spare undershirt. "Will this do?"

She took it with a nod of thanks and waited. It took Crux a moment to realize that she wanted privacy. "My apologies. Let me know if you need assistance."

"Been bathing myself for years. I think I'll be fine." She stared at him until he left.

He heard her dip into the water and did his best not to imagine what she looked like. He had no right.

Fate said he had all the right.

Crux groaned and leaned against the wall in defeat. Fate could say whatever she wanted, it didn't matter if he didn't make a decision.

He wanted Courtney. The feel of her skin earlier in the day had been one of the greatest temptations of his life. And he would have begged fate to make Courtney his. It looked like fate agreed.

But the road ahead would be hard.

And Courtney wanted to go home. To Earth.

Would she ever want to be the dragon queen? How would she react if he told her?

She'd reacted remarkably well to all of the trouble so far, but would this be the one thing that pushed her over the limit and sent her into panic? He couldn't know if he never told her. But keeping this from her felt like a sin.

A fated mate was supposed to be a blessing.

A gift.

And here was Crux, spitting in fate's face.

He didn't know how long he sat there, but it was long enough for Courtney to finish bathing and for Crux to realize just how much his own clothes were covered in muck and, as Courtney said, monster goo. Now would be a good time to clean them.

He skirted around the edge of the fire where she was curled up in his undershirt, her clothing laid out on the rocks to dry. He didn't do anything more than glance at her to respect her privacy.

She didn't look at him.

He deserved it.

Crux stripped off his clothes and dumped them in the spring before diving in after them. Only once he was fully submerged did he remember that he'd given Courtney his spare undershirt and didn't have much in the way of spare clothes to dry himself.

Oh well.

The water was more than pleasant, and Crux floated for a while. He let some of his worries wash away and didn't dwell on the fact that they'd come back as soon as he dried off. He wished he could fully shift and submerge his dragon self. Back home, there was a huge spring that could accommodate his other form, and he'd once spent an entire day in the water.

But this was good.

It would be even better if Courtney was with him. His cock perked up at that thought.

No.

She was his mate. Fate had chosen her for him. But he couldn't make a move until he decided what to do with her. It would be unfair to them both.

That was what his good intentions said. His yearning body told him to damn his intentions and slake his desire. It would feel good for both of them. They needed the release.

Crux sank deeper into the water.

But he couldn't hide forever. And he was hiding. From his mate. Someone he should never need to hide from. He wasn't worthy of the rank of warrior.

So Crux climbed out of the spring and shook himself off like some kind of animal. Then he slipped into his warrior form for just a moment and then back to that of a man. It got rid of most of the water.

There was no such solution for his clothes. He wrang them out until they were no longer sopping, but he didn't want to put them right back on.

He thought he had a spare set of underwear in his bag, but the bag was set out by Courtney. He held his clothes in front of him and stayed on the other side of the fire, just barely reaching his bag to search for what he was looking for.

"You don't have to contort yourself," his mate said. "I've seen naked men before."

That almost had him growling and demanding *who*. But Crux was no fool and he had no right. Courtney didn't know who she was to him. He had no claim on her. And he certainly had no claim on her past.

It didn't mean he had to like it.

He didn't know how to respond to her observation, so he put some of his diplomatic training to use and said nothing. He laid his clothes out beside hers and dug more intently into his bag, looking for his underwear.

"Damn." They weren't there.

"Is there a problem?" Courtney looked at him over the fire, and she no longer looked angry.

Crux lazed back on his rock. His nakedness would have been on display if it wasn't for the fire blocking them. "I'll need to wait for my clothes to dry before I have anything to wear."

"Oh." She looked away, and he was almost certain her cheeks flushed. Then she plucked at the shirt she was wearing. "I can give this back, if you want."

If he wanted. No, he didn't want his shirt. He had another desire entirely.

"Or you could take that off and we'd be equal in our nakedness."

14

THE HEAT that suffused Crux's words was enough to burn Courtney up from the inside. Her nipples tightened, and it would have been obvious if his shirt was anything but black.

She knew what Crux was offering. It didn't have to mean anything. They'd barely survived the day, things kept getting worse, and there was no guarantee that they'd make it out of this planet alive.

But they could spend some time together forgetting their worries, pleasuring each other.

He lay on the other side of the fire like some recumbent king, and it was disturbing to realize that one day he would be. He was a prince. A dragon. An *alien*. And there was lust in his eyes.

For her.

She shifted a bit and became even more aware of

the fact that she was naked except for the shirt she was wearing.

It might be the biggest mistake of her life to sleep with the dragon prince.

Or the biggest regret.

But when was she going to get another opportunity like this?

She still didn't understand what had happened right outside the cave. She could hear the monsters outside screaming and killing, and she was acutely aware of the fact that the evil alien slavers were only a little down the hill from them.

Tomorrow would be a shit show.

More reason to celebrate tonight.

Courtney pulled off the shirt.

The breath that Crux sucked in echoed around the cave.

Courtney grinned at him. "What? Didn't think I would do it?" She lived for a challenge. It was the only way she'd survived so far. She folded the shirt and put it beside her roller skates, not that anyone would judge her if it got wrinkled.

She didn't try to get closer to Crux. She sat back, mirroring his position, and let the heat of the fire soak into her skin. It felt almost as good as the bath in the spring. With another person she might have been self-conscious. She wasn't one to sit around naked all the time.

She could feel Crux's eyes on her almost like a caress, and there was no room for self-consciousness. Not when he was looking at her like that.

"I never know what you're going to do," Crux replied in a cryptic tone.

She wasn't sure how to interpret that. She didn't think she was that far off the mark from a regular woman. She did what a normal person would do, she survived. And without another response on the tip of her tongue, Courtney just grinned at Crux.

The fire flickered between them.

And Courtney took his statement as a challenge. She reached up and cupped her breast, flicking her finger over her nipple before circling her thumb around it, making it come to a stiff peak.

He sucked in another breath.

She shifted until her back was propped up on the wall and then used both of her hands on her breasts, staring at Crux the entire time, waiting to see what the dragon prince would do. She bet the dragon ladies back home didn't do this for him.

Where did the wild stab of jealousy come from?

Courtney shooed it away. Right here, right now, it was just her and Crux. She didn't need to care that he had a fated mate somewhere that he was supposed to be looking for. Right now, he only had eyes for her.

His hand moved, and she was sure he was touching his cock, but the fire was in the way.

"I want to see you," she said. Her breath shuddered a bit, and she was tempted to reach between her legs and stroke, but not yet. They had all night, and nights on Monster Planet were long.

She expected Crux to stand up and move towards her or beckon her closer. She didn't expect him to *breathe* on the fire and shift it towards the back of the cave, where it could still keep them warm but didn't get in their way.

She opened her mouth to ask how, but no words came out.

Crux read the question on her face and grinned. "Dragon."

She'd seen him use his fire powers. *She'd* somehow managed to use his fire powers. And yet it was still difficult to believe whenever she saw him do something impossible like this.

She dipped her hand between her legs, and her fingers came back wet.

Crux moved with a speed she didn't know he possessed and knelt before her, sucking her fingers into his mouth and tasting her.

The way his tongue moved had her moaning, even though he barely touched her. She shifted her legs so that he knelt between them, and his knee brushed up against her sex. She shifted forward for more pressure, and Crux laughed seductively at her seeking touch.

He pulled off her fingers, and his eyes were heavy with lust. Their gazes locked.

They'd never kissed.

She realized it just before his lips came down on hers.

Oh.

It didn't feel like the lust driven kiss of a one-night stand. This wasn't the kiss of a man who'd licked her juices off her fingers. He kissed her with the kind of care he might have reserved for a princess.

He kissed her like she was precious.

And she kissed him back.

Courtney didn't know how she was supposed to kiss a prince. There was probably protocol to be observed. She was probably supposed to call him *your highness* or something equally asinine.

When his tongue stroked against hers, all thoughts like that melted away into a pile of lust. Courtney wrapped her arms around him and pulled him as close as she could get. She needed to get lost in this kiss, to forget all of the bad that waited for them outside the mouth of that cave.

Here it was just her and Crux, two people desperate to feel something. Anything.

Everything.

His cock was hard against her stomach, and Courtney wanted to touch, but her hands were too busy holding Crux to her. It was moments like these she wished she could grow extra arms, just for a bit of help.

But Crux was on it. He pulled away from the kiss, lips wet and swollen, hair mussed, and even more offensively attractive than he'd been the first time she'd seen him.

He had the kind of beauty that made fashion photographers perk up and gym enthusiasts jealous. And at first, he'd seemed untouchable, but now he was pressed up hot and hard against her, and there was nothing untouchable about him.

He dipped his head low until his lips met her breast, kissing around her nipple in the tortuous sort of play she normally hated.

"More pressure," she said. "Do it if you're going to." She didn't want soft and gentle, she wanted something hard enough to leave marks, hard enough to make her remember exactly what she'd done and with whom.

Crux took her at her word, and she gasped as his teeth scraped over her sensitive flesh, the sensation teetering between pleasure and pain. Courtney made a keening noise, not able to articulate anything in words. It was perfect. Any more and she'd pull away, any less and she'd need more.

Where had this man, this dragon, been hiding all her life?

He took his time, sucking and biting and making her body all swollen with pleasure and delight. And just when she was sure she'd had too much, he shifted to her other breast and proved that she could take so much more.

His fingers teased her entrance and came back impossibly wet. And when she started making even more noise, he stuck his fingers in her mouth and made her lick him clean.

From another man, in other circumstances, she might have balked. But Crux was something else.

Some survival instinct pinged in the back of her mind, but Courtney was too high on pleasure to care.

She reached out and stroked his cock, delighting in the sound he made when her fingers brushed against the tip.

But Crux pulled off of her and gave a playful glare. "Don't touch unless you want this all over soon."

"No discipline?" she teased. It was good to hear a man honest about his stamina.

"Too tempted," he admitted before going back to his work of playing her like a fiddle.

But he didn't go back to his breasts. He went lower and proved his mouth was experienced at much more than talking. There was no hesitance, not a hint of it as he stroked her wet folds with his tongue.

Courtney couldn't keep quiet, and from the way he only stroked her harder as she moaned, he didn't want her to.

When he used his fingers with his tongue, she was a goner. She said his name. She might have made promises. She begged for more, all while he wrung more pleasure out of her than she'd ever been given before.

And he wasn't done yet.

"Need you," he said, kissing a path up her belly and rubbing his lips against her neck. He focused there for so long, kissing and sucking, probably leaving a hickey. But there was also tension in his body, different from just the lust.

If she was just a little more focused on him as opposed to what he was making her feel, she might have noticed it.

Instead. she felt him nudging her with the blunt tip of his cock.

"Yes?" he asked, not quite inside her, teasing her like a sadist.

"Oh, fuck yes," Courtney breathed out. She needed this more than she'd known.

He entered her and it was heaven. The stretch from his cock, the way her body accommodated him, the way she suddenly felt *not alone* for the first time in so long. Sex wasn't supposed to be anything but the pleasurable joining of two bodies, but with Crux it was…

Even in her haze of pleasure, Courtney forced herself away from thinking anything that was going to break her heart.

She gave herself over to the sensation of Crux moving within her. Her fingers gripped him tight enough to leave bruises. The hardness of his body and the hardness of the rock under her were a reminder of where they were, but at this exact moment, there was nowhere else she'd rather be.

Crux moved faster.

Courtney urged him on.

She was close to coming apart. It almost felt like she'd be remade by this joining, but right now she didn't care, she just wanted to feel more.

And Crux gave her more.

And more.

And too much.

She cried out again, gasping his name and clutching him as release ripped through her. And not long after Crux joined her, hot seed spilling into her.

She came down from the pleasure slowly and made a sound of protest as Crux slipped out of her. She wanted more. She could handle more.

Her eyes were drooping.

Sleep sounded good too.

But something teased at the edge of her

consciousness, something Courtney knew she should pay attention to. They were both adults, they could handle a bit of fun.

So why was she worried that this would change everything?

15

Courtney woke up first. There was the first hint of light outside the cave and barely any monsters were screaming. Crux lay beside her, flat on his back, cock on display for anyone to see.

Well, for her.

She blushed at the memory of the night before.

And then she turned away.

It was just a bit of sex. People had sex all the time and it didn't change anything.

Yes, he was probably the sexiest man she'd ever met, but that didn't have to mean anything. She forced herself to get up and felt the soreness and stretch in her muscles that was further proof of what they'd done.

If there was a mirror, she was sure she'd see that

she was covered in hickeys and bite marks, more evidence of Crux's… vigorous ardor.

Thankfully there was no mirror.

She splashed some water over her body to wash off as best she could and was relieved to find out that her clothes had dried overnight. Nakedness under the cover of darkness was one thing, it was something else entirely when the sun was high in the sky.

She definitely didn't want the alien slavers seeing her naked.

And right now, she didn't want Crux seeing her naked either.

She'd fallen asleep almost immediately after their love mak—their fucking. They hadn't discussed it. And that was fine. She didn't need to hear him talk about how much he was looking forward to meeting his mate when his seed was dripping out of her.

She put a hand over her stomach and said a prayer of thanks for her birth control implant. That was another bit of stupidity she probably shouldn't repeat, not that they had space condoms.

She had just finished dressing when Crux made a noise and sat up.

"Good morning," he rumbled in that sexy voice of his.

She really had to stop thinking about how sexy he was.

"Morning." She made her voice all business. "Your clothes should be dry and the sun's up. We should get a move on if we're going to steal that teleporter and get out of here."

Crux stood and stretched, his muscles… and his other bits, all on display. Courtney wasn't a nun. She looked, but she snapped her gaze away when he grinned, catching her spying. He walked across the cave without a care in the world, and as he bent over to pick up his clothes, she got a look at his ass.

Damn. Why hadn't she looked last night?

But she wasn't doing that. Last night had been a fluke, and it wasn't to be repeated.

She had to keep that in mind.

"We should move fast. Wouldn't want the slavers to teleport your mate away before you save her." He flinched when she said it. Good. It was a reminder to both of them that Crux had other duties, duties that didn't include fucking a random human.

And it reminded her heart that she wasn't allowed to fall for this man.

Her heart tried to tell her that it might already be too late.

Courtney told her stupid heart to shut its stupid mouth.

Crux cleared his throat as he pulled on the last of his clothes. "About that—"

She couldn't let him talk. If he tried to let her down easy, she would brain him with a roller skate. "Let's go."

Whatever he heard in her tone, it was enough to start moving.

By the time they took down the forcefield and stepped outside, the monster screams were silent. There were two piles of bones right in front of the entrance, a reminder of their brush with death, and strange dragon powers, the night before.

Courtney put it out of her mind. She was ready for things to return to normal as soon as possible.

"How long do you think it will take for me to get home, do you think?" That was her goal. Get home, back to Earth. Forget about the dragon prince and his stupid mate.

Easier said than done.

Crux didn't answer for so long that she thought he wouldn't. Then she realized it was because he was looking out for alien slavers.

Courtney wanted to slap her forehead. They weren't out for a morning stroll. They were in dangerous territory and could be killed at any moment, she had to remember that.

But Crux somehow determined it was safe to talk after a few minutes. "Not too long, if we can get you a trustworthy guide. A few weeks at most."

"My mother is likely to have called in the National Guard by then," she muttered. Not that it would do any good.

"Your mother commands an army?" Now Crux sounded interested. "Are you important on Earth?"

The laugh that came out of her mouth was ugly and full of all the pain that the last years of her life had rained down on her. "Important? Does that make fucking me less regrettable?" She slammed her mouth shut for a moment and then realized she had to keep talking if she didn't want Crux responding to *that* telling statement. "My mother is a lawyer for the federal government. She doesn't command an army, it's just an expression. And me? I'm not important, I'm just a waitress. Thus the roller skates." She held one up as if he needed the reminder.

Crux had a comically confused look on his face. "What do wheeled shoes have to do with being a waitress? Food servers back home wear no such contraptions."

If she was in a better mood, she might have teased him, but she didn't want to play. She just wanted this conversation over with. "Some restaurants use them. I work at a root beer stand. Cars drive up, we skate out with the food, cars drive away. It's a gimmick. And they'll hire just about anyone who won't faceplant while holding a huge tray."

They lapsed into silence as they got closer to the cave where the slavers had hidden for the night. Courtney expected to hear noises from the group, crying women, yelling slavers, footsteps, *anything*.

But it was quiet.

Too quiet.

And when Crux cautiously stepped onto the path close to the cave, he waved her forward almost immediately, and Courtney saw what he was looking at.

Nothing. The slavers were gone.

"Did they teleport away?" The words felt strange on her tongue, another reminder of just how crazy her life had become in the last few days.

"Perhaps." Crux crouched down and examined the dirt. "But not all of them. There's a path leading this way." He pointed in a direction that they hadn't ventured before. It would take them away from the ship and the caves they'd been hiding in.

"I'm game to follow if you are." They needed to do something. "Unless you managed to fix the teleporter we have." She'd forgotten about it after the fight with the monster.

Crux's face went blank, and she could swear he was blushing, but it might have just been the way the light was hitting him. "I didn't fix it last night," he admitted. "I was distracted."

Right.

Distracted.

"Then let's follow the aliens and steal their teleporter."

16

CRUX HAD to find a way to admit the truth to his mate. Her shoulders were stiff and she held herself as if she'd been injured, not as if she'd had the fucking of a lifetime the night before.

The thought that he'd hurt her in some way tore him to shreds, and he didn't know how to make it right. He should have told her who she was to him. He should have made that clear before he laid a hand on her.

But he hadn't. And today he was paying the price.

She wanted to go home. She had made that abundantly clear. And if he forced her to go back with him, he'd be no better than a slaver. If he went to Earth with her, he'd be giving up his crown. He couldn't imagine doing that for someone he'd met two days before.

But how could he bring himself to give up his fated mate?

He followed the trail with Courtney right behind him. The slavers had passed through some time before, and he wasn't too worried about being seen. They walked up the hill for about half an hour before winding downwards.

"Is that a city?" Courtney asked, bumping his shoulder and pointing at a far-off point.

Crux could barely make it out. Courtney's vision was excellent. He squinted and made out what might have been buildings. "Perhaps it's a settlement." He couldn't get too hopeful. But a settlement might have a teleporter, or a mechanic who could fix one. At the very least they'd have food. The meal bars they'd been eating would run out soon, and Crux would love real food. "Let's check it out."

They were going that way anyway; the slavers' path was headed right toward the settlement.

"What's your mate going to be like?" Courtney asked suddenly. The sun was high over head, beating down on them ruthlessly and making them sweat.

Crux almost stumbled at the question. Why was she asking? Did she truly want to know? Or was this some way to torture the both of them?

This would be the perfect moment to tell her the truth.

And the perfect moment for Crux to truly discover how much of a coward he really was.

"She'll be strong in the face of adversity, stronger than she knows. Intelligent. I won't be able to look at her without seeing how much her beauty grows by the moment." *And she'll have a pair of wheeled shoes hooked over one shoulder.* He couldn't bring himself to say that last part.

"She sounds lovely. I'm sure you'll be happy together." Courtney's shoulders slumped even further, and she didn't speak again.

Crux deserved to be pitched into a volcano.

They walked in silence for hours, and at midday, Crux made them stop to take a drink from the canteens and eat the meal bars. Civilization was further than anticipated, and he couldn't help but wonder if it would be better to turn around and give up on this journey.

But they'd gone so far, and with the short days he wasn't sure they'd make it back to the caves by nightfall. Once they were moving again, he kept his eyes open for possible hiding places if they needed to stop for the night.

Two hours later they made it to the edge of the city, their feet aching.

And more disappointment rushed through Crux.

"It's dead," Courtney said. "Ruins."

She was right. Where once a city might have

stood, now the buildings were falling into disrepair and despair. There was no sign of the people who had once lived here.

And no sign of the slavers.

"Do you think the monsters ate these people too?" Courtney asked. "Maybe they woke up in their caves one day and decided it was time to take over." She shuddered.

He wanted to wrap an arm around her to give her comfort. After all, she was his mate, that was his right. But she didn't know who she was to him, and he couldn't say. "It's possible," he agreed. The buildings were made of some kind of sandy stone and looked ready to stand the test of time. There was no way to know if they'd been abandoned a year ago or a century ago.

The sun was starting to set.

This day had been a waste.

"We need to find a place to sleep," he decided. If the slavers were around, they'd need to do the same. And tonight, Crux was determined to use the things he'd scavenged to fix the teleporter and get Courtney to safety. If he couldn't do that, he was calling for help.

They walked the deserted streets, the silence around them eerie in a way it hadn't been while walking the path to the city. Some of the buildings were falling down, others had holes in the walls. But they found a squat building that seemed defensible enough with walls and windows intact.

It would do for the night.

He led Courtney inside and did a sweep to make sure there was no danger lurking and was relieved to find them alone.

"What do you think this place was? A store of some kind?" Courtney asked. There were shelves lining the walls and items covered in a heavy sheen of dust. There were even intact boxes of meal bars, and when Crux scanned them, he found they were safe to eat.

"Might have been. And I'm thinking the people of this city haven't been gone that long," not if their food hadn't turned to dust.

"Do you need to set up the force field thing?" Courtney pushed aside a small table to make a space for them to sit down, then she slumped down to the floor and stretched her legs out, making a sound of pure pleasure.

She had to be hurting after the long day of walking.

Maybe he could massage her pain away.

But he had to answer her question first. "I think the door and window should hold. Looks like they've lasted this long. And the force field could use the time to charge."

"Charge?"

"It recharges when it's not in use," he explained.

"Oh, yeah," Courtney said, nodding, "like a car battery."

He wasn't sure what that meant, but at least she didn't need further explanation.

They shared more meal bars in silence, and Crux cursed himself further. He had to tell Courtney the truth. Even if she chose to go back to Earth, she deserved to know that she wasn't some consolation prize, that he hadn't slept with her to slake cheap lust.

She deserved to know she was special.

He opened his mouth to say something when he heard footsteps and voices outside. He closed his mouth. The monsters screamed, they didn't talk.

But the slavers did.

Crux rolled to a crouch and shuffled over towards the window, waving for Courtney to stay down and out of sight. She interpreted his erratic waving correctly and kept quiet.

Night was falling fast, and the slavers moved at a frantic jog, looking around wildly as if they expected the monsters to come out of every dark corner. They didn't have any humans with them, and Crux was both thankful and disappointed. He assumed that meant the humans had been teleported away.

It also meant he wouldn't have to hold back if they got into a fight.

But the monsters would be coming soon, and he didn't want to fight when the planet's predators might do the work for him.

He also didn't want to give up his hiding space.

Unfortunately, it looked like he didn't have a choice.

The slavers stopped their frantic jog right in front of the building that Crux and Courtney were hiding in. Of course they did, it was the most secure place on the street.

Crux cursed himself for refusing to put up the force field when one of the slavers tested the door and found it locked. That door wouldn't hold up to a lot of force, and he bet the slavers had force fields of their own.

He looked back at Courtney and saw she was standing, her roller skates over one shoulder and his pack secured to her back. "They're coming," he warned.

She nodded.

Crux shifted to his warrior form and moved to intercept the slavers. They weren't laying hands on his mate.

17

FOR FIVE GLORIOUS SECONDS, Courtney thought the door would hold. The evil aliens battered it with a frightening amount of might, and it didn't budge.

Until it did.

The material cracked and the integrity of the door failed. It fell off its hinges and one of the slavers pushed it open.

He didn't last long.

Crux had his claws out and was ready to strike, and strike he did, taking down the first slaver and waiting for the second, but the second was ready for him when he saw his first companion fall.

Courtney hated to sit back and do nothing. She felt less than useless. But all she had was a pair of roller skates and a can-do attitude. That was nothing in the face of aliens with fire power.

Could she do that thing she'd done the night before again? Could she somehow channel Crux's powers and take out the aliens?

She concentrated, reaching deep within herself to find that heat, that fire, that she'd felt the night before.

But she didn't feel it.

Maybe Crux had to be actively using his powers for it to work.

Now was not the time to experiment.

It was five on one now, and though Courtney had the utmost confidence in her man, she knew the odds weren't in his favor. She winced as he threw one of the slavers into the window and glass shattered all around them.

They were making a racket. Night was falling. Those monsters were going to come down on them like a plague.

This was beyond bad.

Courtney concentrated on fire power again.

Still nothing.

She felt the tiniest spark of it when Crux used his powers to blast one of the slavers, but it faded quickly, lending credence to her thought that he had to be using his powers for her to use them too.

She didn't have time to question why she had done it once or if she could do it again. If it came down to it, she would have to, that was her only option.

Crux took out another of the slavers, which meant three were still left. Then she heard the scream of a monster.

She clutched her roller skate. Maybe it was time to start busting heads.

She didn't have a choice when one of the slavers made it past Crux. He shouted a warning, but she didn't need it. She swung out with her skate and whacked him upside the head.

It did the trick and he went down.

A blaster shot nearly took Crux out, but he dodged and sent a bolt of fire at the two remaining slavers.

They went down.

She and Crux stared at each other over the carnage. Now would be a great time for a kiss. But they weren't safe yet.

"The monsters are coming," she said. "Do we have time to put these guys outside before we put up the force field?" She hoped they had enough battery to last the night. There was no time for it to recharge now.

The building shuddered around them, and Courtney looked toward the cracks in the wall where the blaster had hit it. A seam opened up and split, and the building shook.

Crux dove towards her, grabbed her wrist, and pulled her toward the street as the building started to fall around them.

Courtney didn't have time to curse. It was dark. The monsters were coming, and they had no place to hide. She slipped out of Crux's grip and laced their fingers together. This was one hell of a way to die, and Courtney didn't have time to number her regrets.

She wasn't going to waste the few minutes she had left.

"It's been one hell of an adventure," she told Crux. She wanted to kiss him, but she was too scared to look away from the world around them. She wanted to see the monsters coming. She wanted to meet her end face on.

"It's not over yet," Crux said. "Do you have my pack?"

"Yes, why? Do you have another trick up your sleeve?" She might fall down on her knees in thanks if he did.

But Crux shook his head. "Hold on tight," he warned.

And then he proved just what he meant when he said he was a dragon.

He didn't just have claws. He didn't just breathe fire.

He was a freaking dragon.

Between one blink and the next, the man

transformed into a being out of legend, red and gold scales embedded on a black body with huge wings that could surely carry them to safety.

Climb on, she heard his voice say in her head, and she didn't have time to be shocked.

It definitely was not the most shocking thing she'd experienced in the week. She didn't even think it made the top five.

A monster screamed, and it was getting closer. Courtney could see shadows moving at the end of the street.

She clambered on the side of Crux and climbed onto his back, holding on wherever she could. It wasn't so bad at first. And then he moved, and she flattened herself on him, afraid that if she sat up too much she'd plummet to her death.

I won't let you fall, he promised.

"I'll haunt your ass if you do," she muttered.

Monsters were getting closer, coming down the streets and a few on the tops of buildings, but they must have sensed a more dangerous predator in their midst. They didn't charge, not immediately, and Courtney hoped it meant that she and Crux would get out of there without a scratch.

She was being too optimistic.

The first monster charged, and Crux let out a stream of fire, incinerating it.

Now she felt the fire like an inferno in her chest,

and it didn't dissipate when Crux stopped breathing flames.

It should be easier for you to use when I'm in this form, he said cryptically.

If they weren't in the middle of a fight for their lives, Courtney might have asked him to elaborate. But at that moment, one of the monsters on the roof tried to jump on Crux's back.

Courtney summoned his flame by instinct and took the fucker out.

The monsters charged then, not intimidated by the fire but enraged by it. Crux did most of the damage, but he wasn't untouched. At least one of the monsters bit him, and Crux screamed.

Courtney shot fire at any monster that she could see in payback. No one got to hurt her man.

She didn't even try to fool herself into thinking he wasn't hers. He was hers for as long as she could keep him.

The monsters came and came and came. Her world narrowed to burning flesh and fire. On the bright side, she soon became confident enough to move on Crux's back and trust that she wouldn't fall. Strangely enough, it was the muscles that she'd developed from roller skating that helped the most.

There was a break in the fighting. The monsters thinned out for a moment.

Hold on, Crux instructed.

She did as she was told.

And then he pumped his wings and took off, flying into the night and leaving the monsters behind in a search for safety.

1 8

<hr>

THE REALITY of Crux's dragonosity really sank in as Courtney plastered herself to his back and they soared through the air of Monster Planet. The monsters didn't have wings, which was a relief, so there was some kind of safety in the dark night.

But Crux couldn't fly forever. Apparently.

Even dragons needed a break.

They landed high in the hills, ready to blast anything that came close to them. But there were no monsters. And judging by the silence of the night, no other animals either. The monsters must have eaten them all. Or they knew to hide when the sun set.

They found another cave, and Crux shifted back to his human form as if it was the most normal thing in the world. Which, Courtney supposed, to him it

125

was. Nothing lurked in the cave, so they put up the force field generator and started a small fire.

Now would be the time to ask Crux about the fire power. Clearly he knew something about it. And something about the telepathy.

Can you read my mind? She thought the words really hard, squinting at his back.

Crux didn't respond.

Don't ignore me. Can you read my mind? She projected even harder, a vein in her forehead throbbing. But Crux still didn't respond.

Hmm.

"Can you do telepathy with everyone?" She finally used her words, since thoughts weren't working.

Now Crux turned to her. "Only in dragon form. And not everyone." He didn't elaborate.

What was with him and cryptic answers? She needed to know what was going on, why she was one of the people who could read his mind and sometimes use his powers. "Am I half dragon or something?" The thought wasn't quite fully formed when it left her mouth.

And judging by Crux's startled laugh, it was just as ridiculous as it sounded. "I have no reason to believe you're anything but human."

Why did that disappoint her? Okay, Courtney could admit it. She wanted to be special. She wanted

Crux to look at her differently and tell her she wasn't just a plain woman from Earth who'd made stupid decisions, lost an amazing job and the future it held, and was left picking up the pieces while slinging burgers on roller skates.

And she'd probably been fired from that job too.

Courtney decided to give it another night. She didn't want to ask a slew of questions and go to sleep unsatisfied when Crux went all mysterious on her. Exhaustion was already weighing down on her after the hike and the fights, and her eyes felt like deserts from how dry they were.

Tomorrow was soon enough to ask for answers.

It wasn't like she was going anywhere.

She lay down next to the fire and watched as Crux pulled things from his pack. She thought she heard him saying something, but he wasn't speaking to her, and eventually sleep won out and she drifted off.

She didn't dream.

Of course she didn't rest well. She could only take so many nights on cave floors without blankets or bedding before her body started to ache all over. She wasn't built for that. But she was surprised by the light streaming through the cave entrance. It was late in the morning, judging by how bright it was.

Where was Crux?

He couldn't have left her. Could he?

Voices came from outside the cave, friendly sounding. Not like the slavers. Still, Courtney grabbed her roller skates, ready to strike if something fishy was going on.

Outside the cave, Crux was standing beside a woman who was almost as tall as him, with dark hair pulled back in a ponytail and a uniform similar to the one Crux wore, though hers was a lot cleaner.

"This is her?" the woman said, words laced with doubt.

That put Courtney's hackles up, and she swung her roller skate threateningly, not that she thought this woman was really a threat.

"Can you do it?" Crux asked the woman. "And her name is Courtney. She's been through a lot."

A lot didn't even begin to cover it. "What's going on?" Courtney was really beginning to hate surprises.

Crux stepped away from the woman and towards Courtney. "I called in my friend Tracer last night. I couldn't fix the teleporter, but she was able to 'port in based on the location I gave her. She's going to take you home."

Courtney's first instinct was denial. She didn't want to leave Crux behind. Then the saner part of her brain prevailed. Did she really want to stay on Monster Planet? Nope! And Crux didn't want her with him. He had a mate out there to find.

She scrambled for something to say. "You couldn't have called her in three days ago?"

Her dragon looked a bit chagrined. "I thought I could handle it. But after last night… I can't risk you getting hurt. And I have to rescue those women before the slavers fly off. Tracer confirms that their ship is still in orbit. It's time to get serious."

"You're going in alone?" She knew how strong Crux was, but there were dozens of slavers, and she had a feeling he couldn't use his full dragon form on a space ship.

Crux put a hand on her shoulder, and Courtney wished he would touch her more. "I'll have help," he promised.

Something in Courtney's chest cracked, and her eyes were watering. What the hell? Was this relief that she was finally getting away from such a horrible place?

Since when did relief feel like heartbreak?

"I…" She couldn't think of the right thing to say. She wasn't prepared for this. What was going on?

"You'll be safe," Crux assured her. "I trust Tracer with my life and everything precious to me. She'll get you home."

"Will I ever see you again?" It felt horribly needy and revealing to ask, but the words tore out of Courtney, taking a chunk of her heart with them.

Crux cupped her cheek and pulled her close,

pressing his lips against hers in a gentle kiss. It didn't stay gentle for long. He opened his mouth and Courtney swooped her tongue in, devouring him. She wrapped her arms tight around him, as if holding on for dear life would make it so he couldn't abandon her.

Tears leaked out of her eyes, and she didn't care. It felt like her life was ending, and she didn't know how else to deal with it but to put her entire soul into the kiss.

And Crux kissed back with everything he had.

But it had to stop eventually.

They did have an audience.

And this was the end.

Crux pulled back and eventually let go of her completely, stepping back far enough so that he could no longer reach her.

Courtney remained rooted in place. She wanted to beg him to find another way. But she had a life to get back to on Earth, and he had dragon things to do.

"Goodbye," she finally managed to say, and she didn't even need to choke back tears.

Crux just nodded.

Then Tracer powered up the portal and gestured for Courtney to step through.

It was time to go home and leave her dragon behind.

THE FIRST SIGN that everything had gone wrong was when Courtney got to her apartment and one of her roommates tried to slam the door in her face. Tracer had left her behind just down the block from her home and then took off with a casual goodbye.

Good riddance. The woman made Crux look talkative and eager to share knowledge. Courtney was glad to be back on Earth.

For a minute.

"What the hell, Kyle, let me in!" She banged her fist against the door so loud she was sure to annoy Mr. Jareki down the hall, but she didn't care. She wanted a real shower and a real bed and maybe a real meal. She'd been thinking up a story to tell anyone who cared to know for the past few days, but now she was ready to sleep.

Kyle opened the door.

She shared the two-bedroom apartment with Kyle and his girlfriend Carly. They weren't friends, but everyone paid the bills on time and kept the place tidy enough, which was all Courtney cared about.

She wasn't great with having roommates, but she didn't exactly have the income to live alone.

"What the hell?" she asked, shouldering her way into the apartment. "I live here."

Kyle made a noise that had Courtney looking at him strangely. "About that…"

"What?" And then Courtney noticed the pile of things in the corner. Her things. "What's going on? Why did you move my stuff?"

"Did you come to get your stuff?" Carly asked, coming down the hall and flumping down onto the threadbare couch. "It was super uncool to ditch us like that. You owe us last month's rent."

"Hector did pay it," Kyle told his girlfriend quietly.

"That's beside the point." Carly glared at Courtney.

"Hector? What? I leave for a weekend and suddenly you're kicking me out?" Okay, Courtney was guessing on the timeline, but she'd only been with Crux for a handful of days. She couldn't have been gone *that* long.

Though maybe she should have checked a calendar.

"You've been gone a month!" Carly yelled. "No calls. The police came by and said you'd been abducted or something. I knew that wasn't true. Obviously. What are you playing at? Did you go on some type of bender? Have you been sitting in an alley for weeks? Drugs? Is that it?" Carly said it all with stunning intensity for someone slumped on couch cushions.

"Is that what you think of me?" Courtney had never touched anything harder than pot, and she didn't waste money on booze when she was scraping pennies together for rent. Since when was she a drug addict?

"Carly's been binging Law and Order," Kyle whispered conspiratorially. "Don't take it personally."

"Don't take it personally? It's a personal attack! And who's Hector? You guys seriously believe I just bailed?"

The door to her room opened, and a tall man with dark hair came out. He looked groggy and his voice was tired and rumbly. "Can you guys keep it down, I'm working nights this week."

All three of them shot apologetic looks at Hector, who ducked back into Courtney's room and shut the door firmly behind him.

"You gave my room to Hector the Hot Nurse?"

she hissed, keeping her voice down so he didn't hear. "What the fuck? We barely know him!"

"You barely know him," Carly shot back. "He and Kyle have gotten close. And Hector needed a place to stay after he broke up with his boyfriend. We needed the rent money. It's perfect."

"He's in my room. *Not* perfect." Hector was a perfectly nice guy, Courtney was sure, but it was hard to be charitable when he was sleeping in her bed.

"How about this, you can crash on the couch tonight and tomorrow, but we need you out of here by the weekend. Will that be enough time to find somewhere to stay?" Kyle was eager to play peacemaker.

"Kyle!" Carly protested. She and Courtney had never quite hit it off.

Courtney wanted to argue. She wanted her room back. She wanted her life back.

She wanted Crux.

But she wasn't going to get any of that. "I'll be out of your hair as soon as I can," she promised. "But first I'm taking a shower."

Neither Kyle nor Carly argued.

When Courtney was finally clean and ready to start putting her old life together, there was a knock at the door.

The cops wanted to talk to her.

They sat in the living room while Kyle and Courtney retreated to their bedroom. Courtney was on the couch while the two police officers, Marley and Angelo, stood on the other side of the room. Marley had a small notebook in the palm of his hand while Angelo was recording their meeting on his phone.

He wasn't going to get much.

Courtney couldn't tell them where she'd been, and she wouldn't even if she could. She was the daughter of a lawyer, and she wasn't about to talk to the cops without representation.

Marley and Angelo were not happy when she let that be known.

But Courtney sat on the couch and let them talk at her. They gave her more info about her disappearance, and it was dawning on her just how bad things had gone. Like Carly had said, Courtney had been gone for a month. Vanished without a trace from behind her workplace.

Her phone hadn't pinged any satellite or cell tower. She hadn't shown up on any cameras. And there wasn't a trace of physical evidence that gave them a clue of where she'd gone.

The cops had been sure she was dead. People didn't disappear without a trace anymore, it just wasn't possible in a world as connected as the one they lived in.

Hell, they might even believe her if she said she was abducted by aliens. That was more believable than somehow circumventing the surveillance state.

Courtney kept her mouth shut.

Talk of aliens would get her committed somewhere, and she didn't need to add involuntary admittance to a mental ward to the list of shitty things that were happening.

She had to be fired. Her manager fired people for showing up three minutes late. A whole month guaranteed she didn't have a job.

The cops left unsatisfied, and Courtney sank back onto the couch.

Now would be the perfect time for something to go right.

Instead, she shifted, and one of the couch springs poked her in the butt.

Courtney didn't care. She lay down and curled up as best she could. The couch, poky springs and all, was more comfortable than a cave floor. But she would have given it away in a heartbeat if it meant Crux could hold her.

She wanted him so bad it hurt.

How had her life come to this? She'd never depended on a man before, never had her heart set, especially not in a matter of days.

He was a freaking dragon.

He lived on another planet.

Okay, maybe the mental ward was sounding better and better.

Because every moment that Courtney spent away from Monster Planet, the harder it was to grab onto the details. It sounded too out there. A man dragon? Monsters that only came out at night? Alien slavers that abducted humans for their own nefarious purposes?

She couldn't believe it.

She wished that she had something of Crux's, some memento she could clutch so she knew it was all true.

She had nothing. Nothing but memories and impossibly strong emotions. And it would all fade. Courtney had just arrived back on Earth, and it was already fading. One day she'd probably tell herself it was all fake, that she'd had some kind of mental break and imagined a romp with a sexy alien on a faraway land.

But it was real. She was one hundred percent sure it was real.

She shifted on the couch and another spring poked into her. And finally, Courtney let herself cry.

She had no idea what was going to happen. Her life was in tatters, and she'd left her heart billions of miles away.

She drifted off to sleep, wishing she was back on Monster Planet in Crux's arms.

"THESE RAT BASTARDS need to learn how to die!" Doom called over to Crux as he sent a burst of fire at a cowering slaver.

"Is that the last of them?" Crux surveyed the room and saw smoldering heaps of dead slavers all around them. The ship had been full to the brim, and a few of them had even managed to get a few cuts in.

But Crux wasn't alone this time, and he didn't have his hands tied by trying to keep Courtney safe.

He wished with all his heart she was at his side.

"Scorch and Pyro radioed that they've cleared their sector," Doom said as he kicked one of the dead slavers for good measure. "We have control of the ship. There may be some cowards hiding out, but it won't take long to find them."

Doom, Scorch, and Pyro were Crux's friends from

the military academy. While Crux had gone eagerly into the military, his friends were not so excited by the necessary discipline that career required. Instead they took a different path, buying a ship of their own —with a healthy investment from Crux—and hunting the slavers and scavengers who thought the system around their planet made for an easy place to hide out.

They were just the people to call in for this job. They loved knocking heads without asking too many questions. Crux had almost called in his brothers as well, but could only imagine the potential trouble he'd be in with the king if either of them was injured.

No, a pack of bounty hunters made for much better playmates right now.

"I think that makes the ship yours," said Crux with a smile. "Will you keep it? Or are you happy enough with that scrap pile you call home?" He might have been an investor in their ship, but it didn't mean he'd step foot on their deathtrap. He wasn't a fool.

Doom looked wounded. "It has the best upgrades money can buy!" he protested.

"Maybe the best upgrades you can afford. I know exactly how many times your gravity generator has failed." It was practiced teasing, they'd been doing it for years. Luckily Doom wouldn't take it to heart.

"This place is far too big for us. But we'll sell it for

a fair profit. After we return the girls to their rightful homes." He knocked a hand against the hard metal walls and it echoed around them.

That was another reason Crux had called them. There was no risk they'd turn around and try and enslave anyone to recover their costs.

He and Doom took control of the flight deck and waited for the others to join them. It took some time. This had been quite an ambitious run for the slavers, and the number of humans on board was surprising. Eventually, Scorch and Pyro joined them.

Scorch was a tiny warrior, but she'd been the top of their class at the academy. Apparently, she'd been hiding her insolence, because as soon as she was out, she turned into a ball of fury and fire. Her mate, Pyro, was the quieter of the two in most cases, and towered over her, but he flinched away from killing bugs.

Slavers, of course, were another thing entirely.

"What's the report?" Doom asked, sitting back confidently in the captain's chair.

Crux had to bite back a grin. He gave fifty-fifty odds on whether or not the crew actually got rid of the ship.

Scorch hopped up on a desk and let her feet dangle. "Trauma, fear, and anger from the ladies. Luckily no panic. They'd already identified their own leader and started making a list of demands between the time we freed them and killed the last of the slavers. I like them."

"No major injuries," Pyro added.

"We'll need to get a list of where they're all from and if they want to go home," said Doom. "It will probably take a few weeks. I'm scanning the networks for any notes of a bounty on this crew. If not, we'll report for the standard bounty from King Venin."

Scorch groaned. "He never gives enough." Then she shot Crux a look. "No offense, *your highness.*"

"That kind of impertinence would get you whipped by another royal," Crux warned, but he couldn't keep the smile off his face. He was lucky these were his friends. He hated to think how spoiled he would have become otherwise.

Scorch just laughed. She knew he wasn't a threat.

"And what of you?" Doom asked of Crux. "Shall we send you back home safe and sound? Would your father give a reward for your safe return?"

"As my father is the one who sent me on this quest, I doubt it." Crux could step through a portal and be home in a matter of minutes. He'd report to his father and then be exactly where he'd started.

Would he let his father choose a wife for him?

How could he when he knew Courtney was out there?

How could he not when he'd let her go for his—and her—own good?

There was no other mate for him. Fate didn't usually offer second chances, or first ones, at that.

His father would find him a sensible woman, someone likely to be a good queen. And his father was not normally unreasonable. If Crux and this mysterious dragon lady did not suit, he could find another bride. So long as he was actually *looking,* he doubted his father would force him all the way to making his vows.

But there would never be a dragon woman that was good enough, because Crux knew exactly where his mate was, and she wasn't someone his father would ever choose for him.

"Was that a hard question?" Pyro asked gently.

"Let's get the women sorted out." Crux pushed thoughts of his father and his future aside. "I'm not quite ready to go home yet."

You don't have to do this. Courtney whispered the words over and over in her mind as the bus bumped down pothole-ridden streets. She'd managed to find twenty bucks in the pile of crap from the apartment and had promised Kyle and Carly she'd be back for everything once she'd sorted out a place to stay.

And there was only one place Courtney could think to go.

Home.

Ugh.

She got off the bus and waited at the stop for another. Then she changed busses yet again at the bus depot. And that bus put her on the edge of a nice neighborhood full of huge houses and judgmental neighbors.

Home sweet home.

Courtney walked down the sidewalk, a backpack full of basic supplies slung over her shoulder. She'd left the roller skates back at the apartment, and it had been harder than she'd imagined. Those things had saved her life multiple times.

But she was back on Earth. She didn't need a weapon.

That didn't make her relax.

Courtney walked up the long black driveway and then past the manicured garden to the front door. It was just as perfect and sterile as she remembered. She didn't know why her parents insisted on this huge house when they both worked in the city and didn't need all the room.

At this point Courtney was just, well, not happy exactly, but relieved that she had a place to go.

If her mother let her in.

Their last fight had been epic.

Courtney had said things. So had her mom.

And it had been more than six months since they'd spoken.

She wondered if her mom even knew she'd been abducted. Or, well, disappeared. Courtney was the only one who actually knew of the abduction.

Courtney knew she was stalling, so she forced herself to jab her finger against the doorbell and listen while it buzzed. She didn't even know if anyone was home and hoped she didn't have to spend the day waiting on the doorstep.

She buzzed again.

Then she heard footsteps. Her mother.

The woman who opened the door was an older version of Courtney, eyes deeper set and surrounded by thin wrinkles. Her hair was short and sensible, and even though she was clearly working around the house, her clothes were suitable for the workday, though she'd eschewed a suit jacket, thank god. Courtney already felt inadequate, her anxiety didn't need any more ammunition.

"Courtney." Her mother's tone was flat. Not a good sign.

"Mom. Hi." She didn't have a grand plan or anything, and that was looking like a bad thing. Weren't parents supposed to be happy when their wayward children came home?

"I'm not giving you any money."

At first Courtney was sure she'd misheard. Then she blinked hard, hoping she had hallucinated. "Excuse me?"

"I'm not giving you a cent," her mother repeated. "I cannot condone your… actions. You are welcome to stay here until you get back on your feet, but I will be inspecting your things for… paraphernalia. I will not enable you."

"Why does everyone think I'm doing drugs? I've

never done drugs!" Things had gone to shit all because of workplace politics and putting trust in the wrong guy. Then the alien abduction. There was no need for an addiction to make things worse.

"The police came by yesterday. They warned me about you." Her mother crossed her arms over her chest, as if she had to protect herself from Courtney.

"I didn't do anything wrong. Jesus." Courtney turned. She could probably scrounge up a friend—or a mild acquaintance—who would let her crash on their couch until she got a new job.

But Courtney's mom reached out and clutched her arm hard enough to bruise. "Don't you walk away from me."

Courtney stopped. "You're the one calling me a drug addict without a shred of evidence. You're the one who told me it was my fault for getting fired at the advertising firm when my boyfriend stole my project and badmouthed me to everyone. And I was really hoping you could just be my goddamned mother for a minute instead of this judgmental a —*person* but of course you're not. Because I'm not perfect and therefore I'm a failure."

I was good enough for a dragon prince. The thought was a blow to her heart. It wasn't true. Crux had sent her away the first chance he got, and she'd never see him again.

This sucked.

"Just stay until your father gets home. I can give you lunch, how about that?" Her mother's tone turned from accusatory to conciliatory. Maybe she really was concerned for Courtney's well-being. She probably was. She still *was* Courtney's mother, even if they didn't understand one another.

Her stomach growled. She'd felt bad about eating anything at the apartment, though she'd talked herself into scarfing down a yogurt before she could think better of it. She'd left a dollar on the counter as payment. But that had been hours ago, and yogurt never filled her up. "I could eat lunch," she conceded.

Her mother's shoulder sagged in relief. "Of course. I can fix you a plate. I just need you to be honest with me about where you've been."

That was it. Courtney couldn't take it anymore. "You want the truth. Okay. Fine. I was abducted by aliens after work. All I had was my uniform and my roller skates. I bashed an alien's head in with said roller skates. More than one, actually. We crash landed on a planet full of monsters and a dragon prince saved me. Then I got teleported back to Earth where I found out it's been a month and everyone thinks I'm on drugs. Is that what you wanted to hear?"

All the color had drained out of her mother's face. "Oh, baby." She reached into her pocket and pulled out a cell phone. "I think we should take you to the doctor. Um. In case the… aliens… left any probes. For your health."

"I'm not crazy. This wasn't a mental break." But even Courtney could concede that the story sounded crazy.

"I know you're not crazy, honey." Her mom's voice had gone up an octave, as if she was trying to deal with a feral animal.

Courtney turned around to storm away when a bright white gash in reality opened up in front of her and Crux stepped through.

She turned around just in time to see her mother slam the door.

Crux looked at the door and then back to her. "Is this a bad time?"

She couldn't help it. She laughed. Her emotions were a tornado inside of her, and she couldn't make sense of them. "Now I really think I'm having a mental breakdown."

Crux stepped forward and reached out, but stopped his hand before he touched her. "I'm actually here."

"How did you find me?" She had a million other questions, but that was the first that popped out.

He held up the small teleporter in his hand. "Tracer gave it to me. It keeps a record of the bio print of everyone who goes through it. I locked onto your location."

"Oh." Okay. Sure. That made sense. "Why are you here?" Did she need to space-testify in a space-trial of the slavers?

"I had to see you." He wasn't moving back, but he still wasn't touching her either.

"Don't you have a mate out there to go find?" It came out harsher than it should have, but Courtney had been jerked around by everyone since getting back to Earth, and it was time to jerk back a little.

Crux flinched, but Courtney wasn't satisfied with the hit. Then he stood up straighter, like a man going to meet his doom with what little pride he had left. "I lied."

"What?" She took half a step back. "What did you lie about?" Not the dragon thing, that was clearly real. The prince thing? The slaver thing? "What?"

He took a deep, steadying breath. "I found my mate on that planet."

"Then what's the lie?" At this point he was lucky she had decided to leave her skates with the rest of her stuff, because she had gotten really good at busting heads and she was losing patience.

"You're my mate, Courtney."

2 2

———

Crux was never going to lie again. If that was the only way to make sure he never hurt Courtney, it had to be done. Her face had gone pale and her eyes big. Her hands shook, and he worried that she was about to cry. She hadn't looked so scared while facing down monsters, and he hated that he was the one who'd put the look on his face.

"I'm… I'm your… what? No." She shook her head, and her whole body joined the movement, swaying from side to side.

He didn't take it as a rejection. Of course she didn't believe him. He'd done this to himself. "You're my mate. I regret that it took me some time to understand it. And that I didn't tell you. That's why you could channel my power. That's why you understood me when I was in my dragon form. That's why my heart beats for you."

Her breaths were ragged, and she sank down so she was sitting on one of the concrete steps in front of the door her mother cowered behind. "You're lying."

"I'm not."

"I'm human. I can't be your mate." She pulled her knees close and hugged them.

Crux wished he had the right to hold her close. "You are human, and you are my mate. Humans have a funny way of being compatible mates. Your kind is scattered all across the galaxy."

"What?" Now she didn't sound hurt so much as confused.

He sat down beside her, careful to leave some space between them. "You're not the first human to be abducted. Not all of them want to go back to Earth."

She snorted. "I can't blame them."

He continued. "There are human settlements on hundreds of planets. There are probably more humans living in space now than live on this planet. There have been abductions for thousands, tens of thousands, of years. We even have a fairly large community of humans back in my kingdom."

"And the mate thing?" She still sounded disbelieving.

"Humans have been intermingling among the stars for tens of thousands of years. By this point I'm pretty sure most of us have a bit of human in us." It was a fringe theory, but Crux liked the sound of it. Especially when he was sitting beside his human mate.

"You're a prince."

"Your prince." He'd made his decision. If Courtney would have him, he was hers before all other claims. His father would have to agree if he wanted Crux to be his heir. And if not? Well, Crux would figure something else out. As long as he could have Courtney.

"We barely know each other." She kept throwing up roadblocks, and Crux wondered if he had misjudged her emotions.

She still hadn't sent him away.

"We can remedy that. I came here to woo you."

"Woo? Isn't it a bit late for that? We've already…" She gave a nod he interpreted to mean that they'd already made love.

"I've given you pleasure. But I want to earn your heart. Will you give me the chance?" He'd never been so terrified to make a request in his life. He'd run into battle with more surety of his survival.

She reached out and clutched his hand, and the vise on Crux's heart released in relief. "I'm really glad to see you."

"And I you."

"Can I kiss you?" She tugged him close and Crux went willingly.

"You don't have to ask."

Her mouth covered his and he gave himself over to it. It had been far too long—days—since he'd kissed her, and he would never let things get so dire again. This was his mate, and she needed to know just how much she was cherished by him.

He would spend his life showing her.

His senses were a whirr of pleasure, and he would have taken things further if it weren't for something hard hitting him in the back of the head a second after he realized the door to the house had been opened.

"Get your hands off her!" a shrill human voice yelled.

"Mom!" Courtney sprung up and flung herself in front of him. "Oh my god. That's my boyfriend! Stop it!"

Crux picked up the small black device covered in buttons and handed it to Courtney as he stood. "What's that?"

She snatched it away from him and glared at her mother. "A TV remote? Really?"

Ah. Crux understood. It controlled an Earth entertainment system. "Madam," he said from behind his mate, "if I may introduce myself. I am Crux, prince of—"

"Persia!" Courtney spoke over him. Then shook her head. "No, obviously not. That's how we met. He was playing that old game. Prince of Persia. Right?"

Crux's vow not to lie was being tested, but he would follow his mate's lead. And perhaps it was time for him to stop talking.

"I don't know what's gotten into you, Courtney. I think you need help. And, though I hate to do this, if you don't leave, I'm going to have to call the police." She closed the door in their faces.

Courtney slumped back, leaning against him.

"She saw me come through the portal, why should she not know where I'm from?" Crux didn't understand this planet, though he had been given an information packet by Pyro before coming here.

"Because she'll think she hallucinated or it was a solar flare or something. She doesn't think aliens exist. And…" Courtney shook her head and blew out a breath. "It's just not good. Do you have a place to stay? Or were you going to abduct me back through that portal?"

"I thought I would stay for a time." He had a rendezvous with Doom's crew schedule in a few weeks, but he wanted to explore Courtney's planet and win her heart before he asked her to come back with him. "I was given this before I stepped through the portal. Scorch said human cards of credit are very easy to forge." He held up the small plastic device.

Courtney grinned, and it lit up her face. "A black card? Come on. We're going to a nice hotel."

She tugged him down the street, and Crux gladly followed. He had protected his mate on one planet. It was time for her to take the lead here. And there was nothing he wanted more than to explore just what they could get up to together in a hotel.

THE ROOM WAS PERFECT. Beyond perfect. With Crux's black card, Courtney had splurged. They had a beautiful view of the city and the river in the distance. The bed was soft and large enough to fit about sixteen people. There was even a jacuzzi.

It was everything Courtney could possibly want.

But she would have been happy back in that cave on Monster Planet if it meant she could have Crux beside her.

Crux was standing beside the small desk and looking around like he'd never seen a hotel room before. Then again, maybe he hadn't.

"Do you have hotels back home?" she asked, flopping back down onto the huge bed and bouncing a bit.

Crux grinned at her. "There are inns and hostels.

Though my family has properties scattered throughout the kingdom, so I normally have no need of rented lodgings."

"Because you're the dragon prince."

"Because I'm the dragon prince," he agreed. His fascination with the room seemed to come to an end, and he stared at her lying on the bed. "And your mate."

"And my mate." It was still almost impossible to believe. Courtney was just a normal woman. A human. Nothing special. And yet this dragon prince from the other side of space belonged to her. "Come here."

Crux came. He loomed over her for a second before sweeping her up into his arms and crushing his mouth against hers.

It was like coming home.

Everything had been wrong since they'd separated. Her life had gone to shit. Her future was nowhere to be seen. And her heart had been breaking into pieces. Things were still unsure. She didn't know where she and Crux ended up.

But he was here now and he was kissing her, and that was all that mattered.

They were wearing too many clothes. Crux was still in his uniform, though he clearly had cleaned it at some point since their separation. Stripping off body armor when she was determined not to stop kissing him was more of a challenge than it should have been.

And it was a failure.

They finally had to separate to strip themselves, and it only took seconds. No more struggles, no more barriers between them.

Fuck, Crux was hot. He was hot in the flickering firelight of a dim cave and in the bright, sunlit hotel room. Covered in dirt, freshly showered, it didn't matter. He made her heart pound. He made her want.

And she could have him.

All of him.

"Keep looking at me like that and I won't be able to control myself," Crux warned, his voice gruff with desire.

"Is that a promise?"

This time she kissed him, wrapping a leg around his waist and feeling his hard length trapped between them. They tipped back onto the bed and this time bounced together. Courtney smiled against Crux's mouth, horny and joyful and so damn glad she was in this man's arms.

She wanted to be full of him, to be joined with him, and to come with him. She never wanted this feeling of pleasure to end.

And when Crux's fingers teased her entrance, she moaned. He stroked her slick entrance, teasing her with one finger and then another, his thumb rubbing over her nub. Just a bit more pressure and she'd tip over the edge.

But her evil mate pulled back before she crested and smiled against her lips as she made a sound of protest.

"Patience, dear mate," he crooned, rubbing his hand up her side.

"I'll show you patience," she taunted back and wrapped her hand around his cock, stroking him hard and watching as his eyes shut in pleasure.

He jerked in her hand, hips jutting forward in an uncontrolled thrust as he groaned in desire. Then he covered her hand with his own and stopped her. "Not yet," he urged.

"I need you now." Her body was on fire with want and Crux was pushing her down into the mattress. He was so close, and yet they were still that vital distance apart. "Please."

The plea finally got to him, and Crux guided himself to her entrance and gently nudged the tip of his cock inside of her.

How did he feel so much bigger now? That night in the cave she'd been stuffed full and sure he wouldn't fit. And yet now there seemed to be even more of him. Maybe it was the position. Maybe it was the room.

Maybe it was alien space magic.

Courtney didn't care, not as long as she and Crux were together.

He slid into her agonizingly slow and full. It was the kind of torture Courtney lived for, and her body was on fire with her dragon. She wanted to beg him for more, but her tongue was tied up and she couldn't do anything but moan.

It didn't matter. Her mate understood.

He moved in her like he was meant to be there, and she gave herself over to the sensation. She finally knew what it was supposed to feel like to be with someone completely and she was never letting Crux go.

She was possibly never letting him out of this bed.

She moved with him, her body wired for the pleasure they were creating. She was practically vibrating with it, electricity moving through her body and lighting her up from the inside.

It was too much. It was not enough. Courtney wanted more and she wanted it from Crux.

He gave it to her until her breath was coming out in desperate pants and her body rippled in release, holding him inside of her as she came, and then he joined her.

They both breathed heavily as they lay down on the bed. She held his hand, unable to put much space between them, not when she finally had him next to her. It was too perfect to bear.

She was afraid she was going to open her eyes and find out this was all a dream.

"You're real, right?" With another guy, she might have been afraid of the vulnerability that came from asking. But not Crux, not now.

"Absolutely." His fingers squeezed around hers, grounding her in the moment.

"I want to show you my world," she confessed. "But I'm not sure I'm going to be able to let you out of this hotel room."

Crux laughed and then he kissed her.

CHAPTER 24

ONE MONTH Later

Crux loved Earth and all its idiosyncrasies. In a matter of weeks, Courtney had shown him every secret she could, all funded by the strange piece of black plastic that seemed to have a magical power to open up doors for them.

She had asked him who was paying the bill. Crux didn't know. Courtney didn't seem to mind.

But the full moon would soon be cycling back home, and his father would want to see him. And Crux would need to present Courtney.

If they were going back.

The last month had been pure happiness except for one thing. Courtney knew Crux was a prince. She knew he had a duty to his people and his family, and she'd clearly come to the silent conclusion that one day he would have to leave.

He could have told her that he had no intention of leaving without her, but it hadn't yet come up. So Crux hadn't said anything.

But Doom would be bringing the ship around soon, and it was Crux and Courtney's easiest way off the planet. It would take a good bit of maneuvering to get another ride if she wasn't ready to go.

He'd do it. He'd do anything for her.

But the time to talk had come.

"Why do you look like you're heading for execution?" Courtney leaned back on the bed, one of the plush robes the hotel provided wrapped around her. "Whatever you've been building up to, spit it out."

How well she had come to know him in the past weeks. He might as well start at the beginning. "I went to that planet because my father gave me an ultimatum to find a mate, and the matchmaker said you would be there."

"Not quite. If she had given you my name, things might have been a lot easier." There was no malice in Courtney's words. They'd had time to come to terms with their first meeting and how things had ended up.

"Yes, of course." Crux continued. "He told me I had

until the next full moon. And according to my calculations, that day is coming soon. If we want to meet him by his deadline, we'll need to leave Earth now."

"I always knew you'd have to—you said we." Courtney blinked at him a few times and then shifted to get closer to him. "You want me to go back with you?"

"Of course. You sound surprised." Crux cupped her cheek and gave her a quick kiss, but pulled back before he could lose himself in her taste. "You're my mate."

"And human."

"Yes, we've established it." He kissed her again for good measure. "Will you come home with me to meet my father?"

Tension had Courtney strung tight, but Crux didn't let go of her. "I don't have anything to wear to meet a king."

He smiled. "That's easily taken care of."

"What if he doesn't accept me?" Her breath was coming fast now as the reality of the situation sank in.

"Then we leave. We're together in all things."

That shocked her enough to have her blinking hard and staring at him. "You'd—but he's the king. You're a prince. You can't just walk away."

"You. Are. My. Mate." He punctuated every word

with a kiss to her forehead. "We are together. I will not let him tear us apart."

"Is that a big risk?" She flinched as she asked the question.

Crux wished he could reassure her, but he couldn't say how his father would react. No prince had ever brought home a human mate before, not that he knew.

But there was a first time for everything.

"I will protect you. And we can always leave. I promise."

"And if we stay…" It wasn't quite a question, but Crux understood where it led.

"If we stay and my father doesn't do anything stupid, then one day I will be the dragon king and you will be at my side as the queen."

"A human queen of the dragons." This time it was she who kissed him. "A queen."

"My queen." He wanted to see her naked and covered in jewels. He had an entire hoard of them back home.

"Well, you've met my mom. I suppose it's only fair that I meet your dad. It's not like it could go any worse."

Crux laughed and then kissed her, pushing her back onto the bed as the joy of her acceptance burned through him.

Their ride would be there soon, but it could wait while he took his time to claim his mate.

Thank you for reading *Crux*!
I'd appreciate it so much if you would consider leaving a review.
The series continues with *Ranger*.

He's supposed to be a prince, not a prisoner...

Things are as bad as they can get for Ranger when he's thrown in a cell and told he's about to be sold for a profit. But his captors don't know he's a dragon, and he's ready to rain fire on them all in payback.

Until he meets Sidney.

She's stronger than she looks...

When Sidney discovers Ranger on the ship, it throws her world into upheaval. She's no slaver. She'll do what it takes to free him, even if it means crossing her captain and crew. When Ranger turns the tables on her, she's almost too angry to be attracted to him.

Almost.

Freeing Ranger has repercussions. And soon it's

not just Sidney that's in danger, but everyone she loves as well. She'll need to trust the dragon prince if she's going to save them all.

But how can she do that without losing her heart?

INTERGALACTIC DATING AGENCY

LOOKING for love that's out of this world? These strong, smart, sexy aliens are seeking mates from the Milky Way. Just hop onboard with your local Intergalactic Dating Agency. Join our group of authors as we explore the friendly skies and beyond with trilogies of cosmic craving, astral adventure, and otherworldly lovers. Warning: abductions may or may not be included!

Looking for something else? Kate Rudolph has a heart pounding collection or paranormal and sci-fi romance stories for you! Bundles, bears, audiobooks, aliens, and more. Check out your options in the list below. You can find out all you need to know at www.katerudolph.net.

Want to check out one of the books? Click on the series name to find out more!

Dragon Brides

Fated mates, fierce women, and dragon princes.

Crux

Ranger

Saber

Zulir Warrior Mates

Kidnapped humans. Alien Warriors. Electric wings.

The Zulir Warrior Mates series brings you human heroines

and heroes abducted from Earth who find love – and wings! – with the alien warriors who rescue them.

Also available in audio!

Synnr's Saint

Synnr's Hope

Synnr's Spark

Synnr's Kiss

Guarded by the Shifter

Werewolf. Bodyguard. Mate.

The origins of these shifters are shrouded in mystery, but they're determined to protect their mates from any harm that comes their way.

Also available in audio!

Hunting Season

On the Prowl

Stalking Magic

Detyen Warriors

Detya was destroyed a hundred years ago. These

doomed warriors are out to find justice… and their mates.

The Detyen Warriors series brings you kick butt heroines, alpha alien heroes, fated mates, and relationships strong enough to span the galaxy!

The entire series is also available in audio!

Soulless

Ruthless

Heartless

Faultless

Endless

Alien Holiday Romance

Christmas… in space????

These alien holiday romances look beyond Earth's winter holidays and ring in the season across the galaxy! *Select titles available in audio.*

Snowed in with the Alien Beast

The Alien's Winter Gift

The Alien Reindeer's Wild Ride

Trapped with her Alien Mate

Alien Outlaws

Outlaws, schemes, and love… it's all there in the Alien Outlaws series…

Andie Munster is sick of life on Ixilta, the planet she got dumped on after being abducted from Earth six years ago. And when the mysterious and dangerous Xandr shows up looking for a way off the planet, she's half-prisoner, half-co-conspirator in a wild rush to escape.

Rogue Alien's Escape

Rogue Alien's Woman

Rogue Alien's Secret

Rogue Alien's Legacy

Mated to the Alien

Fated Mate Alien Romance

Detyens are doomed to die young if they don't find their fated mates.

Follow along as these mated pairs fight off aliens, corrupt dictators, prejudiced humans, pirates, and more! The books can be read or listened to in any order, though some characters show up in multiple stories.

Select books available in audio.

Pick a book and jump into the action today!

Ruwen

Tyral

Stoan

Cyborg

Krayter

Kayleb

Shayn

Braxtyn

Doryan

Dekon

Stealing the Alpha

The thief takes what she wants, but the alpha keeps what's his...

Join shifter thief Mel as she clashes with lion alpha Luke in an explosive trilogy of two opposites who can't keep away from one another.

Also available in audio!

The Alpha Heist

Entangled with the Thief

In the Alpha's Bed

Save with box sets!

Aliens. Shifters. Warriors. Mates. Get them all wrapped together in these special box sets. Save up to 30% off the price of buying the individual books, depending on the series!

Alien Outlaws: The Complete Series

Mated to the Alien Volume One (also available in audio)

Mated to the Alien Volume Two (also available in audio)

Mated to the Alien Volume Three

Mated to the Alien Volume Four

Stealing the Alpha: The Complete Series (also available in audio)

The Mate Bundle

Detyen Warriors Volume One (also available in audio)

Detyen Warriors Volume Two (also available in audio)

Zulir Warrior Mates Volume One (also available in audio)

Standalone Paranormal and Sci-Fi Romance:

Crashed

Mated on the Moon

Mated to the Alien Dragon

Marked

Bear in Mind

Alpha's Mercy

Gemma's Mate

Find more by Kate Rudolph at www.katerudolph.net